Joanna never expected much from life. She'd had too little affection to believe anyone but her father could ever love her. How could she, when her brother hated her and her mother treated her with scorn?

Then she met Jack. She'd come from privilege, planning on following her father's academic career. Jack came from poverty and abuse, escaping both by serving in the army. A relationship between them would never work. Everyone told her all he wanted was to use her, to get his hands on her father's house. Would he be able to prove them wrong and win her heart? Was she right in trusting her own instincts? If she did, would she be able to hold on to what they would build?

Could she survive what fate would throw her way? War and death, violence and greed, and an attempt on her life would test her strength.

My Father's House

ISBN: 978-1-4874-3389-5
Cover art by Martine Jardin

Published by eXtasy Books Inc

Look for us online at:
www.eXtasybooks.com

My Father's House

By

S D Johnson

Dedication

To my family and Heidi.

Chapter One

Jo

I had to spend Christmas at home by myself. My sister, Fi, offered to buy me tickets to visit her in the States, but I'd only worked at the library for three months. I didn't dare ask for the time off. With the wounds from my parents' deaths still raw, I'd have gladly gone away, but I had no real alternative to being on my own that year.

I'd had an invitation from my brother to visit on Christmas Eve afternoon for sherry. I said no and asked him to pick up his boys' presents from me at the library instead. Guessing he only wanted the presents, I saved him the inconvenience of my visit.

My brother hates the sight of me. He has done since I was in the womb. He is twenty years older, and when my mother found she was expecting me, he helped her set up an abortion at a private clinic.

It's hard to grow up knowing your mother didn't want you, but Charles made sure that happened to me. He relished telling me about the failed plan as soon as I was old enough to understand. It wasn't what any thirteen-year-old needed to hear, but it did explain a lot about the way I was treated at home.

Not only did my mother not want to have me, she also blamed me for the shift in the way my father felt about her. She had got used to my father worshipping her, and when his faith was shaken, she could never restore it fully. She was diagnosed with a heart complaint during the pregnancy, and she blamed me for that as well.

My parents met at a faculty dinner when my father joined the teaching staff of the university. She was the dean's goddaughter and was his guest for the evening. Her background was impeccable, and she was both intelligent and beautiful. She didn't work. She didn't need to. She was active in charity and an essential member of various social circles, and her connections were far reaching. She was a glittering, scintillating presence in those days. Old photographs capture the translucent beauty of her youth.

My father was captivated at first sight. He grew up in Yorkshire, the son of a miner and the descendant of a line of miners and farm labourers. He was unbelievably intelligent and became a classic product of the old grammar school system. He had a passion for history and was the first member of his family to go to university, staying on until his PhD was awarded.

There was no pretence about my father. He was a Yorkshireman who'd happened to find a niche in academia and considered himself blessed. He was in awe of my beautiful, socially skilled mother and was amazed that she had ever considered him as a boyfriend, let alone a husband.

I'm not sure if my mother had a touch of the Professor Higgins when it came to my father, but she decided to marry him and to use all her connections and hostess skills to catapult his career into the stratosphere. She miscalculated slightly, because although my father was passionate about his work and research, he lacked her ambition.

He did love her and allowed her to support his progression to the level he wished to reach. By that time, they had two children, my older sister, Fiona and my brother, Charles. Just as my mother was beginning to realise he didn't share her vision for his future, she had the horror of finding she was pregnant again.

By that time Fiona was at dental school at St Andrews, and Charles was working at an estate agency. She had gotten used to being totally free to do as she wished. She was forty-four and had no desire to be pregnant again. She made an appointment at a private hospital and arranged to have an abortion. Charles was to take her there in the morning and collect her in the early evening. Everything was set for my father never to find out.

I would not have existed if they had had their way. My father found out completely by chance. He had gone back to the house to pick up some documents he'd forgotten. He answered the phone, as no one else was in. He became suspicious when the person on the line would only speak to Mrs. Stephens and would not leave a message or disclose what it was all about.

His curiosity was aroused sufficiently to dial 1471 and press to return the call. He went into a blind panic when he got through to a private hospital, thinking my mother had a secret illness and might even be dying.

In the end, my mother had to tell him what she had planned. Even she could not carry on the pretence of a mysterious illness when he was in such a state.

The wedge came between them then. My father could not believe she had kept the secret from him, could not believe she had arranged an abortion without discussing it, and, most of all, could not believe she had involved Charles in all of it.

My mother, anxious to preserve her husband's adoration, shed tears and tried to get his agreement. She explained, she pleaded, but he couldn't agree, and she was stunned to find just how deeply he felt her betrayal.

I honestly don't know how he would have reacted had she been honest with him from the very beginning. I'm not sure if it was the betrayal or the idea of abortion that made him take a stand, but he held firm. In the end, she cancelled the appointment.

My mother went along with the pregnancy very unwillingly. To be honest, I do understand how awful it was for her to carry a child she didn't want, but I can't wish myself unborn or make myself disappear. It was absolutely nothing to do with me, but when her heart condition emerged during the last months of the pregnancy, my mother came to believe I was totally responsible for ruining her life.

She couldn't bring herself to give me a name. Fi chose it. She had always loved Jo March in *Little Women* and begged them to christen me Joanna. I don't have a middle name. I always thought it might have been March, the way things were being decided, but I spoilt it by arriving in April.

Fi met an American dental surgeon at a conference in London. After a whirlwind romance, she married him, moved with him to LA, and became a partner in his practice. It was a love match and a dream business partnership. Fi had absolutely no interest in her English roots, although she kept in touch with me and encouraged me to visit regularly.

Charles learnt his profession at the local estate agency and set up his own business, backed by my father—at my mother's insistence. He met and married the daughter of one of my mother's cronies, which made her ecstatically happy with Amanda's impeccable pedigree. Amanda was actually the most pretentious person I have ever met, but Mother relished and encouraged her affectations. I did not even make the bridesmaids' shortlist for their wedding. My mother thought it was a wise decision.

My father was my ally as I grew up. He was not naturally affectionate. I don't remember a single hug when I was ill or upset, but he would hold my hand. I knew he loved me. He told me terrifying tales from Greek and Roman mythology in a way that never troubled my sleep. When he visited battle sites or historical monuments, he took me with him, filling my head with marvellous tales from the past.

My mother gave me as little attention as she could get away with, and I grew up thinking I was just an inconvenience because of the way she spoke to me. This was why Charles' revelation about the foiled abortion helped me make better sense of things.

I loved Brenda, our cleaner. She collected me and Beth, her daughter, from school from the first day I started and took us back to her house. We used to play or watch television and then have tea together before my father collected me on his way home.

I used to wish the atmosphere in our house was more like it was at Brenda's, where everyone seemed happy and no one minded if it was in a muddle. We ate tea from our laps in front of the television. Brenda was a warm, friendly woman and hugs came naturally to her. I found myself wishing she was my mother.

I may not have liked the atmosphere at home, but I loved the old house. My bedroom was my haven, and I spent hours in there. I didn't mind being alone. I could close the door, escape into my reading, and switch off from my mother's hostility.

I loved my father's study. Lined with bookshelves, its distinctive odour of old books and leather armchairs always made me happy. I did my homework in there when my father was not at work at his battered old desk. It felt like the safest place on earth.

As I grew older, I became resilient. I always imagined I would make my own way after university as Fi had done. It was inevitable I studied history, and I saw myself following a similar path to my father's, staying in academia until old age.

I was in my third year when I was summoned home. My father had suffered a massive stroke and was unlikely to survive. The family, including Fi, gathered at his bedside, and we prepared ourselves for the worst.

After four days of bedside vigil, my father confounded everyone by regaining consciousness and pulling through. He had lost the use of one side of his body. His speech was unintelligible, but his intellect was intact, which made his condition much crueller for him.

He eventually recovered sufficiently to be moved to the rehabilitation centre in the hospital. Fi went back to LA, and I returned to university. It soon became apparent he would need to go to a nursing home or have full time care at home if he was to be discharged. It was then Charles and my mother started their scheming.

They wasted their time working on me. I'd already made up my mind I would return home and take over his care. I owed him too much to hesitate, but that sort of commitment was beyond their comprehension.

Charles had done the cost calculations for a nursing home and full-time carers and could see his inheritance disappearing down the plughole of fees. The figures filled my mother with such dread the pair of them decided to cajole me into a return home. This was purely to save the cash haemorrhage.

I was on my weekend visit when they launched their charm offensive. The transparency of their approach sickened me. It would have totally dissuaded me had I not been so committed to looking after my father.

We sat round the table on the Saturday evening. My mother, uncharacteristically, had made us tea. The intensity of their flattery was choking me. They kept making the point that the bond between my father and me was so strong I was his best hope of some degree of recovery.

I replaced my cup in its saucer with great deliberation and finally gave them their answer. It sounded more pompous than I wanted, but I was angry. To get my words out without being offensive was the best I could do.

"I have arranged with my tutors to return home at the end of next week. I will complete my dissertation here and submit it electronically. I will need to spend ten days back at university at the very beginning of June to sit my finals, but apart from that, I will take over my father's care."

They realised I had it all arranged. I could see that as well as being relieved over a lot of expense being spared, they were irritated they had not needed to be nice to me.

I spoke of electric beds, hoists, commodes, wheelchairs, and other necessities whilst they sat there, dumbfounded, nodding their heads. The practicalities had escaped them in their desire to get me back to take over his care. I had absorbed all the aids they were using in the rehab ward and had made a mental list.

I said I would talk to the hospital about provision and delivery. I had no idea if this was possible, and I warned them everything would have to be in place before he could return home.

"How much is that lot going to cost?" Charles asked.

"Far less than a couple of weeks in a nursing home," I replied. "Did you think they'd drop him off here. and I'd just haul him about?"

It was clear, apart from the money side of things, they hadn't given any thought to it at all.

My father was not happy about me looking after him. He was frustrated he could not communicate effectively and was annoyed by the incomprehensible sounds he managed to make. "No," was his only intelligible word. He waved his good hand to and fro quickly to signal his displeasure.

"I know it will be awkward for us both, but I want to do it," I said. "We'll get used to it."

We had always respected each other's privacy

scrupulously at our house. I knew it would be embarrassing for us both at first, but he became even more agitated. That was clearly not what was bothering him. He pointed at me and made a U-shape in the air. He pointed at me again and made an M-shape in the air.

I finally worked out what he was trying to say. He'd always wanted me to stay on at university to do a Master's Degree. I took his hand in mine and squeezed it gently, shaking my head at the same time.

"I'm going to finish my dissertation at home, and I'll go back for my finals. I will graduate, but I'm going to look after you. I can always go back and do my Master's when you're more independent."

It did me good to know, even after his stroke, he still wanted me to follow what had been our dream. It reinforced my need to look after him. He deserved it. He sighed heavily, clearly unhappy at the decision.

My mother wasn't unhappy—she was totally delighted. From the first day I was back at home, she seemed to forget that my father was my sole reason for being there.

"I think I'll have a poached egg for my breakfast, with a slice of toast," she said the first morning, and the tone was set. I could have protested. I knew I should have, but I'd not stood up to her in the past, and it seemed an alien thing to do.

I presumed she'd been making meals for my father right up until he had his stroke and for herself whilst he had been in hospital. I don't know why she decided she was too delicate to cook. She'd always enjoyed cooking in the past. She played her part brilliantly, always implying a heart attack was imminent. She had her glyceryl trinitrate spray for her heart to hand all the time, and she wasn't afraid to use it to prove her point. Of course, she reminded me regularly I was solely responsible for her heart condition.

How thoughtless it was of me to have the audacity to have

been born.

I'd only been at home a couple of days when she announced she would be letting Brenda go. Apparently, I'd be able to run the hoover round when my father was asleep. I reminded her I had a dissertation to write, revision to complete, and Brenda had worked for her for over twenty years.

"I don't know what Charles will say," she said when I had finished. "He won't be pleased."

I smiled to myself. Keeping Charles happy was never going to be a priority for me.

We settled into a pattern. I dragged an old camp bed out of the shed and set it up in my father's room. It was much easier than trotting over the landing from my room each time he needed me, but it was an uncomfortable old thing. My hips and back soon became sore.

The days and nights seemed long and tedious, and very quickly, I was suffering from lack of sleep. There is no doubt my dissertation suffered, and I had no one to offer me any help. Charles and Amanda were never going to take a turn.

They telephoned one morning to say they would be dropping by after lunch. This threw my mother into a joyful whirlwind of anticipation.

"I shall want you to go into town," she said. "You'll need to go to Browns to get some of those iced fancies Amanda loves and then to Roomes to get some salmon. You can poach it and make some sandwiches. Whilst you're there, you can pick up a nice piece of plaice for my lunch. Get some coley for you and your father."

She chattered on, thinking of various delights to tempt her beloved daughter-in-law, growing in excitement as the list went on.

My heart sank. I'd been hoping to put the finishing touches to my dissertation whilst the carers were bathing my father.

They came in twice a week to give him a bath and provided the only help I got, apart from the weekly visits of the physio. I collected the bank card and the car keys from the drawer, and my mother looked aghast.

"You're never thinking of using the Volvo? It's only ten minutes' walk into town."

She hated me using the car unless I was playing chauffeur. "I'll be ages. You've got me going from one side of town to the other, and I need to be back in time to cook lunch. You'll have to let the carers in," I replied, not waiting for any more objections.

I passed Brenda in the hall. She had heard our conversation and wasn't pleased.

"They take you for granted," she said. "Why don't you just put your foot down and say no? Poached salmon and a nice piece of plaice for Lady Harriet? I'd feed them on fish fingers!"

I hugged her appreciatively and went on with my errands.

It was hectic that morning. No sooner had I gotten back and checked on my father than it was time to cook lunch. I was poaching both lots of fish in milk while my mother hovered around, supervising.

"You can use the milk to make the parsley sauce," she said, irritating me by stating the obvious.

"Do you think you could go and get some parsley from the garden and chop it?"

She heaved a sigh, collected the scissors, and went to the herb pots outside the back door. She returned with a new mission, which she explained as she chopped the parsley, groaning as if it were hard labour.

"After lunch I want you to get the Worcester tea set from the cabinet and give it a wash. Amanda loves it. It will make tea special."

"No, absolutely not," I said. "I just don't have time. I'll get it out for you to wash if you like."

Clearly, she didn't like that idea and chopped away noisily with undisguised displeasure.

My father's lunch was a blend of boneless fish, mashed potato, and parsley sauce. He was able to manage it using his good hand. He was slow, but it mattered to him to do what he could for himself. I took my lunch on a tray to keep him company.

"We've got a royal visit this afternoon," I told him. He pulled a face, which made me laugh because with one side frozen, it looked funny. He didn't mind. He laughed along with me.

"Are you going to have a nap?" I asked.

He nodded. We understood each other, my father and me. Neither of us were taken in by Amanda's devotion to my mother, and we were thankful she didn't bother to keep up that pretence with us.

They had only just arrived when Amanda insisted she take my mother on a little outing. She thought a visit to La Belle Femme might cheer her up, which it would. It was the most expensive women's clothes shops in the county. My mother became girly and giggly, popping upstairs to tidy herself up and insisting Amanda go with her.

They were soon on their way, and Charles disappeared into my father's study, saying he needed to sort the finances out for him. It was news to me. My father kept his business affairs away from Charles, but I imagined he would have a good pry around. I assumed he could do no harm as I was confident the important paperwork would be in the safe.

I'd checked on my father and found he had reclined his chair and had gone to sleep. I collected my laptop and went into the garden. I liked to sit in the shade under the apple tree with my back against its trunk and lose myself in my work. It was where I'd gone to daydream when I was a child.

I was totally absorbed and did not notice Charles' approach. He startled me when he settled himself on the grass beside me.

"I know you're busy with Pa, but you really need to take care of Ma," he said. "She is very sensitive, you know, and it wouldn't hurt you to humour her a little."

I closed my laptop.

"Surely you didn't need to get her chopping up herbs for you, and you could have washed the tea set, Joanna. It would have given her a lot of pleasure to see it in use."

"Was that after I cleared up the dishes from lunch? Before or after I cooked the salmon for your tea?" I asked. "Or maybe whilst I left our father on the commode?"

"Don't be like that."

"Sorry to remind you, brother dear, but I do have a degree to complete when I have a minute to myself."

"We are keeping Brenda on to make things easier for you," he said.

I looked at him with disgust. I couldn't be bothered to reply. I gathered my things together and returned to the house to set their tea out before my father woke.

Mother and Amanda arrived back as I put the last plate on the table. They were talking animatedly, and both were clutching carrier bags.

"Look, darling," Amanda said to Charles. "Ma insisted on treating me." She pulled a dress from the one she carried and held it against her. She twirled it round her in delight.

My mother looked on with pleasure.

"How lovely," Charles said. He smiled at her with genuine affection. Thinking only Amanda was looking, he tapped his jacket pocket and nodded. I assumed he had found what he wanted in the study, but I had no idea what he'd taken, because my father kept the private stuff in the safe.

"And Ma got herself a gorgeous blouse." She turned to my mother. "Shall we tell them our secret?"

My mother nodded delightedly.

"We had a champagne afternoon tea at La Belle Femme whilst we were there," she said. "It was wicked of us. I do hope you haven't gone to any trouble, Joanna, because I won't be able to eat a thing."

Charles looked at the tea I had just laid out. "If you pack this little lot up, we can take it home for the boys." He grabbed a couple of sandwiches, pushing one into his mouth whole. "Just leave a couple of those cakes out for me."

"I'll get you something to put it in, then I really must go and look in on our father. Will you be coming up?"

"No, I don't want to tire him out."

"Before you disappear, Joanna," my mother said. "Amanda and I have been talking, and we think we should exchange cars. The Micra would be ideal for you to run me about in. I've finally accepted I'll never get my license back. It's sad, but I don't need to hang on to the Volvo anymore."

"The Volvo would be much easier for me now the boys are growing so tall," Amanda said.

Charles nodded. He didn't seem at all surprised this idea had cropped up whilst they were out. The Micra only had two doors.

I had my wits about me that day. "Amanda, could you take my mother out to the Micra to see if she can get into the back?"

"Why on earth would I need to do that?"

"Because we take Mrs. Winters to bridge club, and she wears a leg brace. She wouldn't be able to get into the back."

My mother looked aghast. "Oh, dear," she said. "I can't possibly manage that. My heart, you know. It would be too strenuous." She shook her head. "I'm sorry, dear. It won't work."

Amanda and Charles looked as if they had had their faces slapped, and he glared at me with additional hatred.

I was elated.

The day the results of my degree came through will always stand out for me. I got a call from my university gang at just after eleven. They had been to look at the posted results on the announcements board and phoned me straight away. They were excited, crowding round one phone and all shouting their news at once.

"You got a 2.1," someone said.

I heard that clearly. My heart lurched. It was exactly as I feared. My time away had cost me the first-class degree I'd always assumed I'd get. Expecting a second-class grade wasn't the same as registering it had actually happened. It didn't matter that it was an upper second, it wasn't good enough. My group of friends saw it as a triumph, considering what I'd been through.

"Come over right now," one said.

"Borrow the car and come straight here. We need to party!" another yelled.

I couldn't make head nor tail of who had got what as the chorus of results came flooding over the phone, and I certainly didn't feel like celebrating. I made enthusiastic noises at whatever they said, declined their invitation, and said my goodbyes.

There was no point telling my mother the news, but I went upstairs to see my father.

"I got a 2.1," I said.

He stretched out his good arm and enveloped me in a hug. It was an awkward one, but it remains the best hug I ever had and possibly the only one my father ever gave me. We were totally in tune with my dreams. We didn't need words. He knew I felt I had let myself down, and my hopes were dashed.

I'd needed a first-class degree to stay on to do a Master's at my university and would have to seek admittance in a less prestigious one. I'm sure he thought it was all his fault.

The same day Charles and Amanda came to take my mother into town. They'd said they wanted her to witness their wills, and she was thrilled to be honoured with the task. They were all a little smug when they came back, as if they knew something I didn't

"Charles and Amanda want me to go on holiday with them," my mother said. "We're going to Lanzarote."

I looked at them in amazement, naively assuming this was the sole reason for their smugness.

'You can't possibly go," I said. "Your heart wouldn't take it."

"Nonsense," Charles said.

"I think it will do me good. It's been stressful lately," she said.

I got my thoughts into order before speaking. "You will need to check with the doctor you're fit to fly. It's a four-hour flight, so we need to be sure it's okay," I explained. "You'll need to take out specific travel insurance, too, assuming he gives you his approval. If you don't, they won't pay your medical expenses if you are ill."

My mother, thankfully, appreciated what I had said, but it clearly annoyed my brother and his wife.

"Trust you to put the damper on things," Charles said. "We were trying to do something nice for Ma. She needs a holiday."

You want a babysitter and an open cheque book, my brain replied, but I merely answered, "Don't be silly. I just want to make sure our mother's safe."

My mother ended the conversation. "Don't worry, Joanna. I'll do as you ask. Better safe than sorry."

She liked nothing better than acknowledgment of her delicate health.

Charles was fuming, and when my mother went to the bathroom, he rounded on me.

"You know damn well she just makes a song and dance about her heart when it suits her. She's as right as rain."

Her beloved son revealed his true self once more, and it came as no surprise. I knew she played on her condition, but I'd been with her to her appointments and also knew it was serious, possibly more than she did.

"Then she'll be passed fit to fly, and she'll be fully insured if anything goes wrong. You can't lose."

I went with my mother to see the doctor. He made it clear he would have preferred her not to be taking such a lengthy flight. He said if she used passenger assist on the airline, she should be fine.

The travel insurance cover we arranged proved expensive, but I convinced her should she be ill abroad, she deserved the best care possible. This line of argument appealed to her, and she brushed Charles' opinions aside.

"You can't put a price on good health," she said. "Look at your father."

My father wasn't keen on the idea of her going away with Charles and Amanda. I don't think it was because he was afraid of missing her. She only ever popped in to say good morning and goodnight. I assumed his natural distrust of Charles was the issue. The only way he could show his displeasure was to shake his head from side to side, but he did this emphatically.

Life was much easier for me once my mother went away. Brenda and I shared long chats over coffee as I distracted her from her work in favour of her company. She did me good and reminded me there was a world where common sense existed.

Brenda saw what was going on at our house and had plenty to say. It felt wrong to discuss my family with her, but I needed to talk to someone. I had to have an outlet for all my frustrations. Brenda was the only one I could trust.

"Lady Harriet will soon realise why they wanted her to go on holiday with them," she said. "She's no fool."

Brenda always called my mother Lady Harriet to me if no one was about. She called her Mrs. Stephens to her face. My mother frowned upon familiarity.

She had only been away for four days when I received a call from her. The pretext was she wanted to know how my father was. The fact she had phoned me told me something was amiss, and it didn't take long to discover she was not enjoying her holiday. I was concerned, asked a few questions. and with a little prompting, she launched into a litany of woe.

She was being treated as a glorified babysitter. Charles and Amanda went out for dinner every night, leaving the two boys in the apartment with her. They had pizza delivered for them, which I knew she disliked, and she was having to sit with them, unoccupied, whilst they played computer games.

Apparently, Charles and Amanda were sleeping in after their evenings out, and she was left to provide breakfast for herself and the boys.

There was no lift, and the apartment was upstairs. The steps were external and steep, and the heat made them challenging. She was exhausted and was getting no quality rest.

I took what she said seriously. I had imagined what she would have to put up with from the selfish pair right from the day they'd told me about the holiday. Sadly, it had all come as a shock to her. She had thought she would be pampered and petted. She found herself having to look after everyone and having to pay for the privilege. I had suspected she would be picking up the bill for this holiday. She confirmed it.

"Do you want me to book you a flight home?" I was deadly serious.

There was a pause. "I'd love you to, but I wouldn't manage the journey alone."

"Shall I get someone to look after my father and come out for you?"

There was another pause. "You'd do that?"

"Of course, I would. I didn't want you to go in the first place."

"No, don't leave Henry. It wouldn't be fair to leave your father with strangers."

"Shall I phone Charles and tell him to sort himself out?"

"No," she said quickly. "He'd never listen to you, and then he'd get all moody, and it would make things worse here."

"Then talk to him yourself. Make him understand it's too much for you, and for goodness' sake, cut the purse strings."

I believe this was the longest and most honest conversation I'd ever had with her.

"You're such a good girl," she said. "You've always been kind to me, even though I've been hard on you."

That truly was the nearest to an endearment she ever uttered to me, and I hold it dear to me to this day.

Two days later I got a call from Angus, Charles' elder son. He called me on my mother's phone, and I was stunned to hear his terrified voice.

"Aunty Jo," he said, "Grandma's collapsed, and we can't wake her."

"Where are your mum and dad?"

"Out for dinner," he wailed, "and they're not answering."

"Tell Rupert to go to reception. Get them to call an ambulance. Tell him to say ambulancia, pronto, por favor if they don't understand." I was thinking quickly and speaking confidently, though my heart pounded in panic.

He repeated the words that I prayed were correct.

"Tell him to hurry."

I needed information. "Angus, is Grandma breathing?" She was. "Is Grandma wearing her locket?" She was. "Open it and take the tablet out and try to put it under her tongue."

There was a pause and then he confirmed he'd succeeded.

"Can you find her heart spray?" She usually kept it close. "Squirt one spray in her mouth."

He found it and administered a dose.

Rupert returned noisily to the room to announce an ambulance was on its way. I was relieved to hear those words.

I stayed on the phone and tried to reassure them whilst they waited, at the same time dialling Charles' mobile from the home phone. He picked up at once, presumably expecting serious news from home since I would not normally call him. He was stunned at what I told him.

"Get yourself back to the apartment. Our mother's had a heart attack, and your boys are scared witless."

Thinking back, I was really restrained, but it was no time to express my disgust even though it was choking me.

"Bloody hell," he said. "We're leaving now."

I kept the call going while we waited for help to arrive. The boys were brilliant. Angus stayed on the line with me, and Rupert stayed with his grandma. Bless him. He talked to her reassuringly and held her hand. All three of us were relieved when the ambulance arrived and the men came to the apartment.

It was the most terrifying phone conversation of my life, and I could only end it when Charles and Amanda arrived back to take over. Thankfully, by then, the ambulance staff were in control.

All I could do then was wait for news. I certainly wasn't going to trouble my father just then and bring him up to date, but it was time for me to take him a drink and get him settled for the night.

I could hear his rattly breathing as I neared the door. He had been chesty for a day or two, and the doctor had visited and prescribed antibiotics. It had seemed to be under control, and I could not believe the difference when I went into the room. Could this day get any worse, I asked myself?

He was grey-faced and struggling to breathe, and I had no choice but to call for an ambulance. I sat waiting, holding his hand. He was responsive at first, but he seemed to drift as the minutes passed. I grew more terrified than ever. I kept talking, hoping he could hear me, but I wasn't sure if he could.

He scared me when, from out of his stupor, he suddenly roused and shouted, "Harriet" at the top of his voice and stared round the room in terror, trying to see my mother. He had not said a coherent word other than *no* since his stroke, and now, out of nowhere, he called out her name as clearly as if he'd never stopped speaking. There was a strangeness about that night I shall never forget, beyond the unbelievable events that were unfolding.

The home phone rang as I waited. It was Charles.

"She died in the ambulance. I'll be in touch." It was all he said. I think it was all he could manage.

The ambulance women did not hesitate to transfer my father to hospital as quickly as they could, putting him on oxygen within seconds of their arrival.

I was like an automaton, gathering up his medication and a few essentials and packing them into a bag. I remembered to pick up my mobile, my purse, and my keys. All I could think of was I was going to lose both my parents within minutes of each other. I had no idea what I was going to do or how I would cope.

Charles did keep in touch to let me know what was

happening. He had a lot to deal with. A death abroad brings endless complications, and his boys, not surprisingly, had taken things badly.

In turn, I got in touch with Fi, and she flew straight over. It was good to have someone in the house and be around just for me. She took over the responsibility for everything. The relief and gratitude I felt was immeasurable. I was barely functioning.

We shared the vigil in the hospital to make sure my father was never left alone for too long. He was in a single room, and we both got used to snatching sleep in the armchair by his bedside. We often woke up with stiff necks from where our heads had rolled to one side.

Neither of us were sure if he knew we were there, but it was important to us that we were. Typical of my father, who never wanted any fuss from anyone, he slipped away when neither of us were with him. Fi had just stepped out of the room whilst they turned him. He simply stopped breathing, the nurse said.

All I could think was the tragedy of the total loss of all his integrity and intelligence. I would never hold those large, kind hands again and feel them transmit their warmth and strength to me. My heart ached with loss.

Things had to be done, and I was glad Fi had taken charge. The death needed registering, and the funeral company had to be instructed. Specific arrangements were on hold because we were in the miserable and wretched position of waiting for the arrival of our mother's body from Lanzarote.

Our family was in a downward spiral of misfortune, and it continued. The day before Charles' family arrived home with my mother, Fi got a call. Her eldest son, Simon, had been taken to hospital with meningitis. Within minutes we were booking flights for her. Fi had had limited contact with our parents over the years she had lived away, and she'd been unemotional since she'd got back, but the effect of the news about her son devastated her. It was time for me to take the strain for her.

We clung to each other at the entrance to the airport. We did not have the words to express what we were feeling. Security measures meant there was no lingering farewell, but we both took comfort from that hug because it had said what words could not.

The house felt cold and silent when I returned alone. I gave in and lay on my bed and howled. I howled for my father, for my mother, for Fi's son, for my total aimlessness and loss of direction and, finally, I howled when I realised all I now had for support were Charles and Amanda.

I never wanted to feel such a loss again, and had I known I would, I dread to think what I would have done that night.

Whatever grief Charles and Amanda may have felt had totally disappeared by the time they got back to England. I had been to the funeral home to order flowers and say a last goodbye to my mother. It had turned into a greater heartache than I expected. I was not able to see her.

I had gotten it into my head that I needed to see her to say a final goodbye. When they explained why, it was obvious I was never going to be allowed to see her. I got unusually distressed as the reality sunk in, which made me even worse. I had to get my self-control back before I could walk home.

The funeral assistant made me a cup of coffee and provided tissues. I knew it was part of her job to offer tea and sympathy, but I found her manner extremely reassuring. I managed to recover and head back.

I was in a world of my own as I let myself into the house. It startled me to find my brother and his wife were in there already. Charles was in the study, literally rifling through every file or envelope he could lay his hands on.

"What's the combination for the safe?" he asked.

"No idea," I lied.

I ran upstairs and found Amanda sitting on my mother's bed, surrounded by every jewellery box my mother possessed. She had my mother's pearls against her neck and was admiring the effect in the triple mirror of the dressing table. Fury erupted inside me.

"Put those back."

Amanda spun round. "It's all right, Joanna. Harriet wanted me to have them," she said. "I'm only doing what she would have wanted."

"They're Fi's now. Put them straight back." I was aware my voice was getting stronger and more emphatic. It was enough to bring Charles upstairs to see what was happening.

"What's going on?" He saw the boxes strewn on the bed, saw my face, and knew at once what was wrong.

"Amanda's just collecting what Ma promised her," he said. "You need to calm down. I know it's upsetting, but these things have to be done."

"You two need to understand this, I don't care who promised who what. No one touches a thing in this house until after the funeral," I was shaking with anger. "We will show them some respect. Now, put those boxes away, or I will."

I had never stood up to anyone the way I faced those two vultures, and I know I shocked them both. Amanda started to scrabble to gather the boxes together and return them to the drawers. I turned on Charles.

"You can get the study put to rights, and I warn you, if either of you take so much as a matchstick out of this house until after our parents are buried, I will make you sorry."

I hadn't a clue what I would do or even what I could do, but I must have sounded convincing. Charles went straight to the study and started righting the mess he had made.

I didn't trust either of them. I watched over Amanda until

the last drawer was shut, followed her downstairs, and then went to oversee Charles' activities.

"Just so you know, Joanna," he said as he put the last file back in the cabinet. "Ma changed her will, and she left everything to me. Waiting until after the funeral won't change a thing. This house and everything in it are mine." He slammed the drawer shut.

"I don't give a damn about that. You can have everything, but we will lay them to rest with respect before you two start picking at their bones."

"We can wait, but you'd better start packing your bags. The minute the funeral is over, you're out. We have plans for this place. Big plans."

I wouldn't give him the satisfaction of a reply. I moved to the front door and held it open. I had no more to say, and both of them knew I was not going to back down. I was glad to close the door behind them. I fastened the chain and bolts as noisily as I could to emphasise my point.

It all became clear. They hadn't just got my mother to witness their wills that day. They'd got her to rewrite her own. I determined from then on to leave the chain fastened and the front door bolted. I would come and go through the back door they didn't have a key for. I meant what I said. They were not looting our parents' home until after the funeral, then they could strip the place bare, for all I cared.

There was a lot to tell Fi when she called to let me know that Simon, her boy, was responding well to treatment. Fi was less reserved with language than me. For a good five minutes, the phone line reverberated with a barrage of expletives as she expressed her feelings about our brother and his wife. It made me feel better, and for some reason, when she finished, we both laughed, and we continued to laugh until we could barely breathe.

Grief and shock manifest themselves in the strangest of

ways.

Fi called me back later. She had spoken to her husband and had then called Thomas West, our father's lawyer. He had assured her our father had left everything in perfect order and that Charles was talking nonsense about inheriting everything. That was strange ,because our brother was usually totally in focus when it came to his own interests. Fi said he must have known he was clutching at straws.

I wasn't bothered about inheritances, and now I didn't have to. Thomas West had said he would attend the funeral and arrange a meeting with the three of us afterwards to explain everything.

I would have kissed Fi if she had been with me. All I had needed was someone to ensure the period between then and the funeral was free from Charles and his inheritance hunting. I wanted some peace to put myself back together.

Knowing Fi was going to be able to get back for the funeral was a relief. I wouldn't have to face it alone.

She arrived the day before the funeral, and we were both glad of time together to catch up and get our heads straight.

The next day just the six of us rode in the car that followed the two hearses to the church, Charles and Amanda, Rupert and Angus, Fi and me. The boys were silent and sombre. We made no attempt at small talk, as we each had our own thoughts to manage.

The church was surprisingly full. There was a good contingent of university academics and former students assembled to say their farewells to my father. The bridge club, the Women's Institute, and the Ladies' Conservative Club were out in force to bid my mother goodbye.

They were laid to rest together in one of the few remaining plots in the ancient churchyard, and I was grateful. They were spared the anonymity and vastness of the cheerless public cemetery, where most of the graves lay unvisited.

We moved on to a reception at a nearby hotel, and we three siblings circulated dutifully and accepted condolences from people we only vaguely knew. It was hard to play the part of hostess when trying to come to terms with the burial of both parents and with the impending challenge of the meeting with the solicitor, Thomas West.

He had arranged it for immediately after the wake to let Fi be there before she flew back home the next day. Simon was recovering, but she did not want to be away from him for too long. She also had little interest, or so I thought, in the estate we were to discuss.

I braced myself when I saw Charles greet a latecomer, as I assumed this was his solicitor. He arrived with a folder of documents and sat on one side as the last of the guests left. We then withdrew to the meeting room Thomas had reserved, and we seated ourselves in silence around the conference table.

Thomas West took charge immediately. His opening remarks destroyed Charles' devious machinations once and for all. "Your mother pre-deceased your father by nine days, and by the terms of her most recent will, everything she owned then passed immediately to your father. Therefore, your father was the sole owner of all their joint assets at the time of his death. His will applies, not your mother's, and I am here to inform you all of its contents."

He eyed Charles' solicitor from beneath his enormously bushy brows. "Do you have any objections?"

Charles watched anxiously as his solicitor scanned the paperwork in his folder. He took his time, putting up a pretence of equality with the older, more assured man.

"No," he said. "I have advised my client that this is the case. He wishes me to point out Mrs. Stephens made it clear in her will that, upon her husband's death, all her possessions should transfer directly to her son Charles, and we can be in no doubt those were her last wishes."

Thomas West looked at him with total contempt. "Are you saying you will be contesting Mr. Stephens' will? It is my duty to advise you, in my opinion, you have no case in law."

The solicitor knew only too well and made the best he could of the impossible situation my brother had put him in. He looked uncomfortable but said he had been asked to speak on behalf of his client. He said Charles wished to uphold family honour by respecting the wishes of our mother.

"Exactly," Thomas countered. "Mrs. Stephens bequeathed everything to her husband in her latest will. Her husband outlived her. We shall follow his instructions as the law dictates."

We listened to the detail of my father's will in astonishment. We discovered the house was solely owned by my father and always had been from before they were married. We'd never known that. Though it made no difference to the outcome, it crossed my mind that maybe that lovely old house might have helped pique my mother's interest in my shy and retiring father. I pushed the thought away. It was not the day for spite.

My father left the house in equal shares to the three of us with the proviso that if any of us were still resident in the house at the time of his death, they should be able to stay on until their circumstances allowed the house to be sold and the proceeds divided.

There was a sum of money invested for property repairs and maintenance, but the rest of the money was to be shared equally between the three of us. There was an exception to all this. Charles had received a loan of £150 000 from my father. This had to be repaid, and he discovered he now owed Fi and me £50 000 each.

I have never seen my brother look so shaken. I truly think

he'd believed my mother had persuaded my father to write the debt off. He'd also been banking on my father dying before my mother, which made the holiday he'd wangled out of our mother so ironic.

My mother's personal jewellery was to pass to Fiona, and I was to receive my paternal grandmother's wedding ring and locket. I was relieved. These arrangements had been discussed with Fi and me long before Charles had tried to interfere. Beyond that, there were small, very specific bequests to Amanda, Angus, and Rupert.

Thomas West had not finished.

"Fiona has made it known to me she has no interest in the house. Without knowing the content of the will, she instructed me to transfer any share of the property she might inherit to Joanna. I will follow her wishes in due course."

"Bitch," my brother said.

I didn't know if he meant Fi or me. He probably meant both of us. I was as shocked as he was and had no idea Fi had been speaking to Thomas West beyond making arrangements for the reading of the will. It appeared I was going to own two thirds of my father's house and could live there as long as I wished.

"This whole thing is a farce." Charles slammed his fist on the table. "There was nothing in my father's will about repayment. I have a copy right here."

He took a document from his breast pocket and brandished it at Thomas West. "It's her. The conniving little cow must have forged it." He was pointing at me by then.

I now knew he had taken our parents' wills on the day of their visit. I wasn't sure why they'd not been in the safe, but I could remember his smug face when he tapped his pocket to let Amanda know he'd been successful.

Thomas West raised his eyes to the ceiling in exasperation. He sighed and then spoke slowly and clearly, as if he was talking to an idiot. "Your father added that codicil to his will the day I drew up the loan agreement for him. It was signed and witnessed. It stands in law."

I was embarrassed to be seated at that table. It was impossible to understand what Charles had been thinking to create a scene on such a sombre occasion. Fi, aware of my discomfort, gave my arm a reassuring squeeze.

Charles rose to his feet. "I will be taking advice." he said. He looked at his solicitor with contempt. "From someone who knows what they are talking about." I saw his solicitor raise his eyebrows at Thomas West. "This is a viper's nest, but you lot won't get away with it."

He left the room, slamming the door with such force the pictures rattled on the wall. We were all stunned and sat in silence for a couple of minutes.

Fi was the first to recover. She shook hands with Thomas West and thanked him.

He acknowledged her thanks and then took my hand, holding it with both of his. "Do not let your brother try to intimidate you. I am here to uphold your rights, and you must contact me immediately if there are problems."

I thanked him, and after he left, I implored Fi to change her mind about the house, but she was not interested in it. Her life was in LA and had been for many years. She wanted to do something to secure my future, and I was both moved and grateful.

We walked out through the reception room where Angus and Rupert were sitting on a bench seat, all alone. There was no sign of Charles or Amanda.

They ran to me, both in tears.

"We did our best, Aunty Jo. We really did," Angus said, still clearly tormented by what they had witnessed.

Fi and I opened our arms and the four of us hugged each other. For the first time that day, we all allowed ourselves to cry.

Fi and I returned to the house by taxi, both emotionally drained. As we climbed out, we saw a man with an electronic device apparently sizing up the frontage and another armed with a camera taking pictures of the property.

"What the hell are you doing?" Fi demanded.

"Mr. Stephens has instructed us to put the property on the market. He said you'd be back around now and would be able to let us in."

The photographer extended a business card, which Fi tore in two and threw to the ground. "Fuck off," she said.

The man looked confused.

"You heard me," she said. "Fuck off or I'll call the police."

She opened the front door, stood aside as I entered and then slammed it shut behind us. I was glad she'd been with me, and I thanked her again and again. My nerves were taking hold.

"It's a good job I was here," she said. "You'd have let them in and made them a cup of tea."

Once again, we erupted into hysterical laughter, more as a release of our stress than amusement. When we calmed down, we realised we had different interpretations of Charles' behaviour.

"Are there no depths too deep for our brother?" Fi asked. "The scheming little bastard."

"I'm not so sure. It was ridiculous to try to put the house up for sale. He's not behaving rationally, and it's not like him. I think he truly believed he could get us to uphold Mother's will."

"You're too soft. You're used to letting him walk all over you."

I disagreed, but I wasn't going to argue with her. The day had been stressful enough.

Fi went back to the States, and I was left alone. I had some decisions to make. I couldn't go back to continue my studies, as I'd ended up with a second-class degree. My university demanded a first class one to allow me to proceed. I was feeling too raw to go through the process of an appeal on compassionate grounds.

I loved my father's house. I didn't want to leave it whilst I was emotionally shaky to move somewhere to continue my studies at a different college. I needed to find some work. My father had left money for maintenance, but I needed money for food and to pay the bills.

I applied for various jobs including classroom assistant, bank clerk, and library assistant. I went for whatever was advertised. I wasn't in a position to be fussy. Unemployment was so high it was a tough time to be trying to find work, but the sudden retirement of a library assistant on health grounds threw up an unexpected opportunity. I started work more quickly than I could have hoped.

Being busy stopped me from brooding over the recent misfortunes my family had faced. It also engaged my brain as I came to terms with the resources the library held and became engrossed by the local history section. I had had no idea what a wealth of treasures they held.

No one else at the library shared my enthusiasm. They left the local history section to me pretty swiftly. This was how I came to be reacquainted with Marcus Burrows.

He had once been one of my father's students and had gone on to work for him in the history department at the university. He had had a meteoric rise and had been my father's successor, becoming the youngest professor on the campus.

A lot of speculation had developed back then about his sudden departure from the university. My father believed grief was behind it. Marcus had been married to an internationally renowned geneticist, and she had died very soon after being diagnosed with a particularly aggressive cancer. She had been a brilliant and vibrant woman, and my father thought Marcus Burrows' move into research was an emotional retreat.

He'd started a genealogy research business as a side-line. He needed the income to supplement the grants he managed to access to underpin his research.

We never discussed any of this. We got to know each other because I'd been able to access the documents he wanted far more quickly than he was used to. He always made a point of asking for me. We bonded over our love of history. I started to undertake some smaller genealogical investigations for him. They kept me busy at the weekends, and I was grateful. There was little else to occupy me.

I appreciated his kindness. He came round and set up the software on my laptop and provided me with a colour laser printer. We put everything in my father's study. Marcus commented it was strange he could still feel his presence in there. I knew exactly what he meant.

He went through the process of how to create a portfolio for the customers. He never seemed to mind the calls I made to him when problems cropped up. In fact, he always seemed pleased to hear from me. I presumed it was affection for my father causing him to be kind to me. My father had had a way of gaining genuine respect from people.

Despite all this, Christmas was approaching, and I was bracing myself to spend it alone. If I was being honest, Christmas had always been a slightly underplayed event at home, and there was no sense of being deprived of fun and festivity. Despite that, the empty feeling of spending Christmas totally alone was having a depressing effect, and I dreaded its arrival.

Chapter Two

Jack

I was going home for Christmas for the first time in years. I'd got three weeks' leave, and I planned to get down to the library and do some family history research. You'll understand why it was important to me when I've told you a bit about my family. I wanted some proof there was something good and decent in the past.

We had a good start though. Our dad was a scaffolder and was well paid. We lived with him and our mam in a nice house in Alberton. If you know Tremby, you'll know Alberton's a decent enough area. In those days, all the houses had clean windows, net curtains, and tidy front gardens. That's what Danny, my brother, told me.

I always drive back to my old family house when I'm in Tremby. I sit outside it for a while, telling myself I once had a good home, my father's house. A place I don't even remember living in.

Danny has told me about those days many times. He was inside that Christmas. He had had a successful garage business going for a few years, but it wasn't totally legit. He used it as a front and stole high quality cars to order. He did very nicely until he and his partner, Leroy, were caught in a police sting. If he had still been at home, it wouldn't have been quite as bad.

I love my brother. I can't tell you how many times he looked out for me and how many beatings he took for me from Jim, our stepdad. Danny's much cleverer than me. If things had turned out different, he could have done anything he wanted with his life, but he never stood a chance. He always did his best to make sure I was all right.

Danny always says our mam and dad were like Romeo and Juliet, they were so much in love. Apparently, they used to leave soppy love notes to each other all over the house, and Dad used to bring Mam flowers on a Friday when he got paid. My brother swears our mam used to look after us properly then and was pretty. I think these memories make Danny have a soft spot for our mam, and I don't. I don't remember those days.

Our dad was killed in an accident on site when I was three and Danny was six. Things went wrong from then. Our mam just couldn't cope without him. From what Danny says, she started drinking at the funeral and didn't stop. She got compensation from where dad worked, but she burned through it. Danny says we never saw any of it, and he had to beg her for a couple of quid to go to the shop to get us something to eat. He says we lived on dry bread and jam and crisps.

At six years old, my brother was looking after me because our mam was either at bingo or blind drunk. We were stinky kids in those days. Mam rarely remembered to do the laundry, and Danny was too young to sort out how to use the washer. We were too young to give a damn about having a bath, and it never occurred to her we were a bit rank.

Anyway, she stopped paying the mortgage, and in the end, we were evicted. We would have been on the streets but for Jim. She'd met him at the bingo. Danny can remember him coming to our house and staying over. I can't. I can't even remember living in our old house. I only know which one it was because Danny had showed me.

I knew I'd be going back to look at it at some point whilst I was at home. I always hoped I'd remember something when

I sat outside it in my car.

I was nearly five when we lost our house and our mam moved us in with Jim. I remember because I started school at the same time. Jim's house was a three bedroomed council house in the backstreets. It was a strange design, identical to every house in the neighbouring area. The bathroom was on the ground floor, next to the kitchen, providing the only toilet.

Our mam and Jim shared the big front bedroom. Danny and I were put in the box room, sharing a single bed. I wondered why our room was called the box room when there were no boxes in, yet the middle room was full of boxes, piled high. I learned later Jim fenced and stored goods for a number of the neighbourhood thieves.

Jim had three old cars on the front where the lawn had once been. All stood on bricks. What was left of the privet hedge had gone wild and straggled over on to the pavement, where two wheels of his on-the-road vehicle always stood. Passers-by had to walk into the road.

We did get fed at Jim's. Mam was too scared of him not to put food out at tea times. Danny used to get cereal for us both before we went to school while Mam and Jim were still in bed. We were on free meals, which meant we got a hot meal each school day. In those days no one bothered making sure schoolkids ate healthy food. We got lots of chips followed by stodgy puddings swimming in custard. We knew no better then. We enjoyed every bit and had seconds whenever we could.

Jim was an idle, scrawny, sharp-faced man who spent most of his time lounging on the settee, either watching the racing or daytime television, but he was vicious when he was drunk. He was knocking our mam about soon after we moved in. We used to lie in terror in our bed and listen to the shouting downstairs. It wasn't long after that he started on Danny.

Danny took his beatings in sullen silence, but when we were alone in our room, he would tell me his plans. The day when he knew he could take Jim on and win would be the last day Jim would ever touch him or mam. He promised me he would never let him hit me, and he kept his word.

If Jim lashed out in my direction, Danny would push me out of the way and take the blows. I learned to run upstairs and slither my way under our bed and press myself against the wall to make sure I was out of reach. I would lie there in the fluff and dust, sweating with fear and listening.

My heart would thump away as I heard Jim swearing and pounding away at Danny. Danny never made a sound. I think if he had, Jim would have had the satisfaction of hearing him whimper, and the beatings would have been over quicker, but it was Danny's way of showing contempt and defiance.

Danny used to tell me more of his plans as we lay in the dark. He was going to get a job at Royces in Derby, a good job on the shop floor. He would get us a place, and we would be all right then. I loved Danny with all my heart, and I believed every word he said.

By then, I was supposed to be reading every night with my parents. Danny could read well, and he would listen to me struggle away every night. I can't pretend we read any more pages than what we had to, just enough to keep the teachers happy. By then, Danny could forge our mam's signature on my record sheet. It was no use me asking her. She'd just tell me to sod off.

Both of us went to school when we were feeling rough. It was better there than it was at home. If ever either of us was really too sick to go, Danny would write the absence letter. We knew our mam wouldn't. It kept the teachers off our backs. No one ever questioned his attempts because our mam's hands shook so much by then her writing looked like a child's.

Jim expected our mam to do his washing which meant, as long as she remembered, she would throw our stuff in with his. It sometimes hung outside on the line for a couple of days, but at least it had seen water. It never saw an iron, but we didn't know about ironing then, so we didn't care.

Strict about Friday bath-night, Jim would run us a bath before he and mam went to The Crown. He said he had to do it because he wasn't paying for us to waste hot water. He would throw a rag of a towel through the door, shut us in, and leave us to get on with it.

We hated the run from bathroom to bedroom, clutching our dirty clothes in front of us, because there were always some of Jim's so-called business pals around. They had a way of leering at us as we ran past, making us both feel uncomfortable. This was the system Jim imposed and neither of us dared challenge it in those days, even though it humiliated us both.

We would rush to our room, drag on our clean pants and tee-shirts, and listen for the shout from below. The words never varied.

"You can get downstairs, you little bleeders, and clean that filthy bath."

We would run downstairs, and Danny would scrub the bath. We were using either Vim or Ajax in those days, which is why the bath always felt gritty when you sat down. I can remember the scratchiness to this day.

My childhood memories aren't great, but Danny's are far worse. I know he resented it all, but he never complained. He pinned all his hopes on getting a job at Royces and finding a place for us to share.

It was about a year after we'd moved in with Jim when the first baby arrived. Danny told me there was going to be one because our mam had a fat belly. He knew about those things, but I don't know how.

As far as I can remember, Kylie came howling into the world and screamed for the next year when she was joined by the twins. They screamed even more than she did.

There were some temporary rearrangements as Jim moved Kylie into our room, and Danny and me into the middle room along with the boxes. It didn't make much difference to us. We still had to share the same single bed as there was no room for anything else. It was harder to sleep, though. We were nearer to Jim and our mam, so we could hear the twins crying in their room on one side and Kylie screaming on the other.

Jim bought a caravan when Samantha arrived, cleared the cars off the front garden, and installed Danny and I into the ramshackle wreck that became our home. Danny was ten, and I was seven when we moved in. It became our haven. It was boiling hot in the summer, but we left the door and windows open all night. There was nothing worth stealing in there. It was freezing in winter. In the end, we shared the same bunk and huddled together for warmth.

By the time Danny moved to the senior school, a tattered old building way past its glory days, he had given up. So had the teachers, a weary team of defeated individuals who expected little and accepted even less. Danny's books were never marked and each year his neat writing of September had turned into a wayward scrawl by October.

He was mixing with the older kids, messing about with them after school. His speech by then was littered with the words we heard Jim hurl at our mam, only Danny wasn't using them in anger. He was still looking out for me and would come to the caravan to share his booty, liberated from the various shops he and his pals passed on their way from school.

"Nix-pence," he would laugh, as we stashed the biscuits and chocolates we couldn't manage to eat under our bunks.

Danny was smoking by then, and I wanted to copy him.

Jim smoked, our mam smoked, and every visitor to the house smoked. It never occurred to me I wouldn't smoke, and one day Danny gave in to my constant pleading.

He passed a lighted cigarette to me across the gap between our bunks. I took a hearty drag, and I coughed so much I dropped the cigarette. It fell on to the cheap bedding and set it alight. Danny was out of his bunk immediately and got the fire under control by grabbing the cover off me and stamping the flames out. I know he burnt his feet. I saw the sores, but he never said a word or complained. He got rid of the charred cover and replaced it with one he sneaked from the house, and no one was ever the wiser.

Actually, I was a lot wiser. I never smoked from then on. I'd frightened myself to death and had no wish to choke myself again. It didn't put Danny off, but he realised it was better to smoke outside, away from all the cheap and clearly highly flammable coverings that decorated our van.

Danny was drinking, too, but he never offered me any. He wouldn't let me near it. I had no wish to try back then. My mam was a shaking wreck because of the drink, and it turned Jim into a vicious bully. It frightened me, and I was glad Danny seemed the same whether he drank or not. I didn't realise what Danny was getting his hands on wasn't very strong. He wasn't drinking enough for it to have a major effect, but it made him feel grown up.

We were happy enough in our caravan, but we had to pull our weight with our sisters. We both became expert at nappy changing and preparing bottles. When we were in the house, we usually had a baby over our shoulder or in our arms. We became expert at feeding and burping them.

To us, they were the babies, chores that needed attending to if we were in the house. We didn't bond with them or play with them. We dealt with them as best as we could. Sometimes I feel guilty now about it, but we had no guidance, no nurturing model to follow. We knew nothing about kindness

Jim was a sperm donor, not a father, and our mam wasn't capable of nurture. After the fourth girl arrived Jim took it upon himself to "get the snip." I didn't know what it meant, but Danny said he'd had his willy cut off. It seemed a bit far-fetched, but Danny was usually right.

Whatever it meant, Jim lounged around on the settee like an invalid for weeks, and we had to run around after him as well as the girls. Mam was in her own world, staring into her glass most of the day and only energised when it was time to go to the Gala Bingo or The Crown. At those times, she would sweep a wonky line of red lipstick across her face and drench herself in the cheap perfume she got off Atherton Market.

"You look like a million dollars," Jim would say.

At those times I really wanted to believe he loved her, though her bruises contradicted any such thoughts. Danny and I were needed then, too, because we were the babysitters. We could not crawl back to our caravan until they got home at whatever time they chose.

I was often found asleep at my desk after those nights, but no one at school was bothered.

Life muddled on for us all. Christmases came and went as far as Danny and I were concerned. There were never any presents for us, though we had the joy of seeing what Jim acquired for the four girls. They received whatever was the hottest toy of the season. Sometimes their presents arrived ready wrapped, direct from under someone else's tree, courtesy of one of Jim's friends.

Danny and I enjoyed one Christmas more than all the others. Jim was going to provide storage for a line intended to make him a fortune in the run-up to Christmas. All the traders on the markets who were linked into the opportunity were ready to start shifting Santa Towels.

As we helped unload the boxes in the dead of night, stacking them to the ceiling in the front room, Danny kept snorting. I knew something was making him crack up, and I couldn't wait for him to let on when we got to the caravan.

I had a long wait as he was convulsed with laughter and couldn't tell me for at least ten minutes. Jim's pals were not the best readers, and the eagerly awaited Santa Towels they had stolen turned out to be products for women. When Danny had explained the joke to me, I laughed, too, even though I was a bit put off by what he'd said. It did play on my mind for a long time, but then his chuckling became so infectious I had to join in, chortling away until my sides ached.

It took us ages to go to sleep when we'd put the light out because, just as it went silent, one of us would say "Santa Towels" and we would set off again.

It took us all our acting skills to look astonished when the error was discovered the next day. To be honest, if Jim hadn't cleared off to bed and left all the unloading and stacking to us, he could have stopped the drop right away.

"You stupid pair of buggers," he moaned. "You silly looking sods. Fancy not reading the labels."

"We couldn't read them with the lights off," I said, risking my own neck for talking back. "We just had the landing light on like you told us."

I'm sure Jim knew it was all down to him. Danny didn't get the back of his hand, even though plenty of insults were flung our way.

We had to move the telly into the kitchen for our Christmas viewing as the delivery was a slow-mover and the front room stayed out of action until nearly Easter. Jim saw sense for once and didn't expect Danny and me to get rid of any, though our mam was roped in to shift some packets down at the bingo.

I remember those days really well. That's when Danny got interested in girls. He got sufficiently interested to want to sneak them into the caravan.

Now, I worshipped Danny, and I agreed to go in the house when he let the first one in. I waited until she had sneaked out before going back. I wanted to know why he had wanted me out of the way.

"Sorry, bro," he said. He had started to adopt the language of the streets, and it still sounded strange. He explained the mysteries of reproduction to me that day to let me know why I couldn't be around when he brought a girl back.

"If that's what you want to do, I'll always let myself into the house and keep out of your way. If you have a girl here, I'll make myself scarce. I can always say we had a ruck."

He nodded and fist-bumped me. We were a team, no matter what. I just wished he'd apply for the job he wanted at Royces, but he never mentioned it from then on.

When Danny was in Year Eleven, he'd started going to the boxing club in Atherton. I knew, but no one else did. He was learning his craft and biding his time, all the while hiding his smouldering resentment for Jim.

Done with school by then, he'd grown hostile to any show of authority. He was always in some sort of trouble. He never did any homework, though he would help me with mine. He was clever, far cleverer than me. If he'd have knuckled down, he could have passed all his exams. As it was, he didn't even bother to turn up for them. He was also resigned to the fact there would be no apprenticeship for him at Royces in Derby and no little flat for us.

He'd made no effort to find a job, and the pair of us idled our way through the summer holidays. We had just finished eating our dinner one day, and we were going down to Atherton Park later in the afternoon to hit a tennis ball about and meet up with some of his mates.

"You need to get your arse round to Frank's," Jim said,

plonking his pots on the table. He always ate in the other room, watching the telly. He said the rest of us were like pigs at the trough. He'd only come in the kitchen to deliver this order.

"Why?" Danny asked.

"Because I bloody well said so," Jim said.

I could see Danny's anger rising.

"Frank wants you to play decoy. He's got a quick in and out job lined up for this afternoon. He's got it all figured out. He conned an old girl into getting her guttering fixed last week. All you have to do is knock on the door and say your dog's got into the back garden."

Danny stood up slowly. "I'm not going to help him rob some old lady."

He worked to his own code of ethics and would only steal off people he knew could afford it or deserved to stand the loss.

Jim pulled his arm back ready to strike and grabbed Danny's tee-shirt at the neck. Danny was too quick for him. He landed a punch with his right on Jim's jaw, knocking his head sidewards. Jim let go of the tee-shirt. Danny followed up with a barrage of swinging fists, left, right, left, right, left, right.

To be fair, after the first, heavy blow, Danny just demonstrated his speed and accuracy and did little harm with the flurry. He was letting Jim know what he was capable of. Jim was howling, sprawled on the floor, as much from shock as anything. Mam was screaming, and the girls were crying. The kitchen resembled bedlam just then with all the noise and the overturned chairs.

"Don't you ever lay a finger on me or our Jack ever again," Danny said. "If you do, I'll kill you."

I really believed he meant it, and a chill went through me. Danny was my hero, and I didn't want to think him capable of killing. It did show me how much I meant to him, and it made me love him even more.

"Let's go," Danny said to me, as if nothing had happened, and I followed him like an obedient puppy, glad to get out.

I was bursting to talk about what had just happened, but Danny didn't want to. I realised then he didn't like what Jim had turned him into, but as he always did, he was looking out for us.

We walked over to Atherton Park in silence, and I was starting to worry about him but as we neared there, Danny cheered up. "We'll go in the Co-op as we pass," he said. "I need a drink."

I knew the drill. We did as we always did and came out with a bag of crisps each that we paid for and a stolen bottle of cider stuffed up Danny's bomber jacket. In Danny's world, you could steal off the big shops and use young lads to act as decoy, but you didn't steal from small shops or old ladies.

I was thirteen by then, old enough for Danny not to mind if I drank a little. His mates never showed, so we laid about under a tree and shared the cider. I was glad it was just us as I needed to talk, and the cider had loosened my tongue.

"I think I'm gay," I blurted out. I had a vague idea if you weren't obsessed with thinking about girls and sex you must be gay. I found the idea of girls, their periods, and sex totally revolting.

He looked at me as if I was crazy. "Don't be such a prat," he said.

I had started to tell him, and I needed to get the rest of the worries off my mind. They had been plaguing me for weeks.

It had all started after what Danny had told me about women and their periods on the Santa Towel night, and I'd struggled with the disgust I'd felt since. It had got worse after the night when he brought that girl home. If that was what it was all about, then I wasn't interested, yet every boy in my class seemed totally obsessed. I'd decided I must be gay.

Danny listened. That was what was good about him. He always listened, and he never laughed. I could only ever have talked to him about it.

"Do you like boys?"

"Of course I do. I've got loads of mates."

"I don't mean like that. Do you think about kissing them and everything?"

I looked at him as if he was crazy, and he saw my ignorance and innocence in that single glance.

It was time for another one of our Danny talks. God bless him. The way he took responsibility for me makes me cry every time I think of it. As I listened, I wondered how he'd come to know so much, and I knew so little, when we both lived in the same home and went to the same school.

What he told me put to rest all my fears. I was definitely not gay, but the way he told me about homosexuality made me realise what a sensitive person he was under all his roughness. He made sure I understood it was okay if that was my choice.

"We may as well finish this bottle," he said, holding it up to the light. "If we go home roaring drunk today, no one's going to say a word."

"They wouldn't dare," I said, thinking how much I loved my brother. A grin spread over my face. "And I'm not gay!"

"It wouldn't matter a damn to me if you were," he said, and he hit me in the loving way he always did when I was being daft.

That afternoon, in our cider haze, we felt good.

We both knew Danny's dreams of a job at Royces had come to nothing. He had left school with no qualifications, and no one would give him a reference. He had to make his own way in the world, so he took a job stacking shelves at Asda. His pay wasn't going to get us a place, and the job was driving him crazy.

I started to build dreams of my own. The army had been in for a career day at school, and from then on it was all I wanted to do. I was doing all right at school, and I realised I could have a career in the army. I liked the idea of building a future because I had nothing going for me in the present.

I went to the Army Recruitment Office the next week, got a positive response, and went back to the caravan loaded with leaflets and my head full of information. I don't think I stopped talking for half an hour as I told Danny everything I'd found out.

"We can join up together," I said. "We can get away from round here and start again, just like we always planned."

Danny looked at me as if I was mad.

"You know what I'm like when someone orders me about. I wouldn't last five minutes."

He didn't give it a minute's thought, and yet, he could see how much it mattered to me.

"We could be together, and you could get into engineering." I pleaded then. "We'd get somewhere to live, and all our meals, and it would be just what we've always wanted."

He shook his head. "Not for me, Jack."

At that moment it felt like the first time Danny had ever let me down, and I was angry. I let him know. Looking back, I was behaving like a selfish prat. It was my dream, not Danny's, and it never could be. He'd had to be too self-sufficient to want to give up his independence. What I didn't realise then was that my reaction hurt him.

He didn't say anything, but he grabbed his bomber jacket and threw it across his shoulders.

"I think I'll crash at Leroy's tonight," he said. "See you tomorrow."

"Yeh!" I replied. "Get a place for you and him while you're

at it."

Looking back, I'm ashamed of myself. I didn't realise it, but my words had stung him into action because after that he and Leroy started to think ahead. They went cold-calling for days and eventually got themselves taken on as apprentices at a garage off Britannia Drive. They were both car crazy, and they'd put their heads together and come up with a plan that would work for them.

When he finally turned up at the caravan again, he told me about the new job he'd landed. By then, I'd realised how stupid I'd been, thinking Danny could have made a life for himself in the army, and I was glad to hear his news. He was as excited as I'd been when I got back from the recruitment office.

He'd brought a bottle home for us to celebrate. Leroy came round, and we shared it. Neither of them mentioned their long-term plan, but it was the start of a partnership that would last for years and see them both end up in jail. If they'd have known that as they sat in the van that night, laughing and joking, I swear they'd have still gone ahead. They shared some good times for a few years and knew they were owed them. They'd both been through a lot.

Danny and Leroy got themselves a flat on Leicester Road as soon as they got some money together. When he left home, he never said a word to our mam or Jim. He just walked away, with one bag of belongings slung over his shoulder. It's a cliche, I know, but he never looked back.

By that time, I was sixteen and had managed to scrape a clutch of decent qualifications together. I was ready to make a move. Danny backed me as I applied to join up, and he forged mam's signature of consent on the paperwork. He borrowed Leroy's suit and went with me to my interview, explaining he was there because our mam was too sick to go with me. He made a good impression, but that didn't surprise me. Danny always could turn on the charm.

Basic training took six months, and I can't pretend we kept in touch all that much. Lads don't, do they? I let him know when my passing out parade was and arranged for his ticket to be left at the gatehouse, just in case.

I never heard from him, but that day, as I stood on the parade ground and surveyed the crowd as best I could, I saw him, dressed in Leroy's suit once more.

The hug we shared when it was all over brought us both to tears, though we pretended it hadn't. We had time to have a drink together and exchanged what news we had. He had nothing to tell about our mam and the girls. He hadn't seen them since he left home.

He didn't stay long. He'd pinched a car to get over to me, and he wanted to ditch it at Nottingham on the way home and complete his journey on the Red Arrow. It was funny to feel as proud of him as I did that day, despite the stolen car. He'd done it all for me, and there was no one else in the world that day who gave a damn.

I'd been away over ten years. The girls had grown up in that time and things had moved round in the house. Kylie was in the box room with her baby boy, and the twins and Samantha had got the big room. Jim and our mam had moved into the middle room.

The twins, Leanne and Dionne, were working the local markets. They sold cheap cosmetics and perfumes. They shifted whatever Jim and his mates passed on to them. Kylie was living on the social and waiting for a house.

When I looked at the three of them, I could understand why girls had never really interested me. Those three were all from the same mould. They all had thin, ratty hair they scraped tight into a bun thing that made their faces looked stretched. These buns, on the very top of their heads, wobbled as they spoke. They had long and lurid false nails, and they all had heavily pencilled brow lines that were drawn far too high. They looked perpetually inquisitive, which was stupid as they rarely managed a thought between them.

I'm not sure if they shared their wardrobe, but their outfits were totally interchangeable. They wore white jeans or leggings—I don't know which—but they were always too tight. The tops they wore always flopped off one or other of their shoulders, and when they went out, they would put on short furry jackets. It crossed my mind that the twins might be buying their clothes in bulk off other market traders, but I never asked them. I wasn't that interested.

Samantha, the youngest, was trying. She was working as a care assistant in a home that had opened round the corner. The other three had grown into feisty, foul-mouthed young women, well-able to look after themselves. Samantha had to wear a nursing type of uniform for work and wasn't allowed to wear make-up or have painted nails. She'd got herself a boyfriend and spent most of her time at his house. She was doing her best.

Our mam was in a bad way. She was as skinny as a bird, with bony, shaky hands. She spent all day in the front room watching the tv screen. Jim chose the programs, and I'm sure she had no idea what was on. They both chain smoked, and the room was continually thick with a cigarette smog that caught your throat as you went in.

Mam didn't go to The Crown or bingo anymore. She wasn't steady enough on her legs to leave the house. The girls said she'd got dementia, and although she'd not seen a doctor, it seemed a reasonable assumption.

Jim didn't seem bothered that mam didn't look after him anymore because he'd got the girls waiting on him. He still went out at night, and Kylie was sure he was seeing a woman at bingo and paying her home visits. I think he'd given up lashing out at the girls because it was clear they'd fight back. Judging by her lack of bruises, my mam was safe from his temper then.

I must have been mad to spend that Christmas at home. I'd always gone away with my army mates, but it had been a funny year. Richo and Tommo had found girls to settle down with and were spending Christmas with them. I could have gone away on my own, but I didn't fancy doing that. It wouldn't have been the same without them.

I'd called in to visit Danny on my way home. He was doing his time in Nottingham Prison. He was surviving and had no complaints. I tried to get to see him every couple of months, and obviously, I was his only visitor.

He had put on a bit of weight, which made him look better. His face was less drawn. He wasn't getting the exercise he'd been used to and was eating regularly, causing the pounds to creep on. He'd been in a bit of bother for sticking up for a couple of under dogs, but that's what I'd expected of him. He was no longer on good behaviour standing, which meant I couldn't put money into his prison account for tobacco and stuff anymore.

He was always pleased to see me and eager to hear about life in the army. It made me feel good that he was still interested in me, and he was stoked that I'd made corporal. I wondered if he ever regretted rejecting my pleas to join the army, but I daren't ask. He wasn't talking about the future. He never had much to say. His life was limited, and he'd still got a couple of years to serve, but I was always glad to spend an hour with him.

He said I was stupid to be going home for Christmas, and when I went into the caravan, it was obvious he was right. It hadn't been used since Danny and I left, and it smelled fusty.

The heater had a lot of dust to burn off, and the smell was so bad I ended up with the door open. I wasn't bothered about that. I'd spent many nights under the stars out in the wilds on exercises. I was pretty hardy. I just felt the bleakness of home wrap round me and drag me down.

I'd made my plans, though. I was pinning my hopes on finding something good about my dad's lot. Danny had always told me what a great guy he was, and I'd reached a stage where I needed to know for sure I wasn't trash.

I didn't tell the family. Jim would have been furious and would have had plenty to say about how much he'd done for me. My mam and the girls wouldn't have cared less. I didn't need their indifference rubbed in my face.

Danny was right. I was an idiot to go home, but I was there I had to make the best of it.

Chapter Three

Jack

I could have worked in the caravan, but apart from being chilled by the damp, the rain hammered on the roof non-stop, and the light was bad. It was better at the library than it was at home. I hadn't been in a library for years and was stunned by the lack of books. It had become more of a resource centre, and most of the space was taken up by computer workstations. It saved me some money, though, as I got free access to all the ancestry sites.

The clientele was more dead-end than I expected. I guess those guys had no regular access to either warmth or Wi-Fi. It struck me I could have been one of them if I hadn't joined the army. When I remembered Danny, wasting his days away in jail, it made me realise I really had nothing to moan about.

Women had never really interested me much. I guess growing up alongside my shrieking sisters and alcoholic mother made me doubt there was a fairer sex. My two army mates had both got married, which, as I said, was why I ended up at a loose end this Christmas, but their women were mirror images of my sisters and definitely not the type for me.

That was why I was surprised to feel stupidly self-conscious when I saw the young woman who worked in the library. I first noticed her when I logged off my workstation, stood up, and backed straight into her. I nearly knocked her off her feet as she was walking by. Our two worlds collided with a resounding bump, but she was fine about it.

From then on, I started behaving like a total kid, watching her whenever she wasn't looking my way, and then jerking my head back towards the screen if she turned towards me. I'd seen my mates act this way at school, but it was new to me, and I felt stupid.

I noticed an old guy came in nearly every day. She spent a fair bit of time getting stuff out for him. They seemed to have a lot to talk about. I noticed the way his eyes followed her, and it struck me he had it bad. I realised I was jealous. Just like that. Jealous of an old guy in a library because I wished she was talking to me, not him.

I remembered the old conversation with Danny when I said I thought I was gay. It's funny how these things come into your mind, but in the library that Christmas, I was emphatically not gay. The thought made me smile.

The next contact I had with her was when she had to come over to reboot the machine when they all went down. As she leaned over the machine, I recognised the floral scent she was wearing as lily of the valley. They used to grow like weeds round the caravan, and I always liked their smell. I searched my brain for something cool to say, but nothing came to mind. I simply thanked her.

She smiled at me, and I was overwhelmed by how naturally beautiful she was. Her skin was glowing without a trace of makeup, and it struck me how much I hated the caked-on stuff the women I knew wore.

From then on, my mind was occupied by schemes of how I could get to talk to her. Then it struck me. I'd ask her how to follow up the leads I'd already discovered about my dad and see if there were any articles in the local papers about his accident.

She was unbelievably helpful. My dad's accident had happened so long ago the newspapers from then were only available on microfiche. She got the right rolls of film out and showed me how to set them up on the reader. She showed how to get photocopies of the stuff I wanted. As she did all this, I was able to read her name badge without being obvious. Joanna Stephens.

She seemed genuinely concerned this was going to be the first time I'd seen these reports and stayed until I'd accessed the pages I needed. She was right to be concerned. As I came face to face with a photograph of my dad, my hands shook and sweat poured from my face.

I was twenty-eight-years old, and I had never seen a picture of him before. There he was, in grainy black and white, looking the image of Danny. It was like looking at someone I'd known all my life. I felt a burst of anger directed at Jim for making our mam throw out all the photos of her and my dad as well as the ones of Danny and me as kids. What right did he have to try to destroy my past?

The newspaper had done a couple of stories arising from his accident, including one about his funeral. I'd been there, but I had no recollection, and now I was looking at a picture of his coffin and seeing it as if for the first time. I had not expected it to be emotional, and I had to wipe my eyes with the back of my hand.

The library girl came back with a glass of water and a couple of paper tissues, then disappeared without a word. I was glad of them and took several minutes to sort myself out.

I browsed on through the obituary they'd published and was shocked to see the photograph of my mam and dad they'd used. Danny had told me about how gorgeous our mam had once been, and he was right. She looked like a film star in the picture, and I shuddered at the thought of the dried up, shrunken woman she'd become. She was looking at my dad with adoration, and for the first time in my life, I felt sorry for her.

I'm not making excuses, but I had never understood how

hard losing her soul mate had been on our mam. I'd only been a kid, and I'd given it no thought. The mam I knew hadn't cared about anyone.

The obituary revealed my dad had been a keen footballer and had played in the Sunday league for a local team and had once had trials for Nottingham Forest. Danny would be stoked about that. He was crazy about them.

The girl came back and sat at the side of me. She'd come to check if I was okay and seemed really interested when I showed her my photocopies. I felt a bit odd. Half an hour ago, I'd been thinking up ways of getting to talk to her, and she was there listening to me telling her, through my sniffles, what I'd found out about my dad.

I'm glad she did. No one else would have given a damn.

Why was I spending ages choosing which shirt to wear? Why was I annoyed I'd left my good aftershave in my quarters? I was only going to the library, for heaven's sake.

I was going to research my grandparents. They'd cropped up on the ancestry site I was using the previous day, but I hadn't had time to investigate them properly. I was also kidding myself. I was hoping to get talking to the library girl, Joanna, again.

Kylie was hammering on the bathroom door, but as I hadn't been home for over ten years, I decided she could wait another couple of minutes.

"It's not as though you're even a paying guest." She scowled at me as I came out.

I blew her a kiss.

"Piss off."

My classy family, I thought.

Actually, I did pay. I chipped in £50 every month to Samantha's bank account towards their bills, but that was for the two of us to keep from the others and Danny to grumble about. It was an emergency measure. They'd kept getting their gas and electric supplies cut off and turning to me to bail them out. After it had cost me a few hundred a couple of times, I'd realised involving Samantha would be easier.

I also put £50 into an account each month for Danny, ready for his release, but he didn't know about it. He wouldn't be pleased, but he'd need it.

It was easier to get some food in town than share the kitchen with the tribe and fight for the last drop of milk to put on my cornflakes. The White Horse did a good cooked breakfast and decent coffee, so I made my way there.

The hard-core drinkers were there already, occupying their usual chairs and stools. Some were studying the horses' form in the Racing Post, but others were staring into their pints and waiting for the new day's intake to kick in. I'm sure it's the same in the pubs that open early in every town.

I thought, there but for the grace of God . . . even though I'm not religious. Once again, I was grateful to the army for saving me from that life.

To walk from there to the library only took ten minutes. That included a stop to pick up a notepad and a decent pen on the way over. Knowing I was on the brink of finding out where I came from excited me, but not as much as I was to see Joanna Stephens, the library girl, again.

She smiled when she saw me, and I took it as a good sign. I logged on and got into the ancestry site. My grandparents were there, waiting for me to find them, and I opened my notebook ready to record their details. I was relieved to confirm there were some respectable folks in my family.

Their wedding certificate revealed my grandfather was a carpenter and joiner, and my grandmother was a secretary. They were real people with respectable jobs. My grandad had his own business, and I found him in the yearly trade directories as W.S. Wicks, Carpenter and Joiner.

I was stoked with the news but less happy to find their death certificates. I had only just found out about them, only to learn I'd never get to meet them. I chased up their death certificates quite easily.

My grandmother died of breast cancer at forty-two, and my grandfather died of lung cancer at fifty-three. They'd have known about Danny but not about me or my dad's accident. Danny didn't remember them at all, which made me wonder if he'd spent any time with them. He'd have been their only grandson. I hoped he did.

My dad's side of the family don't seem to live long. At least, their deaths explained why they didn't step in when my mam went off the rails. They could never have helped Danny, me, or my mam for that matter. This made me feel better, because I always wondered why they'd done nothing. It meant it wasn't that they didn't care.

Danny had already told me he remembered our other grandma coming round loads of times after our dad died, but our mam either wouldn't open the door or stood on the step and screamed at her. The last time she came, our mam had gone for her with the floor mop and chased her down the path. Danny said she took a good few whacks to the head and never came back. He had no idea why they were at loggerheads.

I never intended looking into my mam's side of the family, so I wasn't going to find out why. It was my dad I wanted to find out about. I was doing fine. I'd already established he had no brothers or sisters. I had no aunts or uncles lurking about with secret pasts. I either needed to go further back on my grandad's side or start looking into my grandma. I decided to stick with Grandad Wicks for a bit longer.

I was reading through my notes when she came over. The delicate smell of lilies of the valley told me she was near. Colour rose in my face as I turned to look at her. She'd brought over the copies of the various birth, marriage, and death certificates I'd paid for online and had sent to the printer.

"You're getting somewhere," she said, handing them to me.

I nodded, "It's turning out better than I thought."

"Do you want to check for announcements in the Evening Post?" she asked. "I can work from the dates on the certificates."

I checked my watch, "Could we do that after lunch?" I knew from yesterday how long it might take, and I didn't want to miss out on the opportunity to spend time with her later.

She looked at the wall clock in surprise, as if she had no idea what time it was. "Good heavens," she said. "My break's in fifteen minutes."

Now, I'm not the smoothest mover when it comes to women, but I had to take my chance. "Can I buy you lunch?"

She looked surprised, and I thought I'd blown it as she took ages to reply. It wasn't the most enthusiastic response, but it was good enough for me.

"Why not?" she said.

Jo

My mother would have fainted if she if she had seen me in the cafe chatting away with a soldier. She hated tattoos, and Jack Wicks had two full sleeves of them. His hair was cropped close, almost to the point of baldness, and it made him look hard.

He spoke with the local accent, which she hated. She had spent my early years correcting any lapse in my pronunciation, loathing the flattened vowels I'd picked up at school. He came from Atherton. Just the name of the area would have made her raise her eyebrows. She had always approved of men in the military, but only those with a commission. Jack would not have been welcome over her doorstep.

I wasn't deliberately rebelling against her prejudices just for the sake of it. I found him genuinely interesting and sweetly old fashioned. He'd held doors open for me, moved my chair in and out for me, and had helped me with my coat. I also liked the way he seemed a little flustered and lacking in confidence, as if he was anxious to make a good impression.

I'd tried come to terms with being totally alone. Was I clutching at a straw? Was I being what my mother called desperate? Maybe, but Jack Wicks was kind and friendly, and right then, I was grateful for the company. The run-up to Christmas is a bad time to be alone. The people at the library were lovely but a good generation older than me. They had busy lives, homes, and families. They had people to share a drink with, to go to the theatre or cinema. No social outings were ever arranged from work.

Yes, Charles had invited me over for sherry on Christmas Eve. Who asks their younger sister over for sherry? It just meant I wasn't worthy of a seat at their table for a meal. I'd refused his invitation, and he'd picked up my gifts for Angus and Rupert, which I suspected was all he wanted. He'd thanked me and told me to have a good Christmas. That was kind of him, my loving brother. What did he think I'd be doing alone at home? You can't even pull a Christmas cracker when you're on your own.

The thought of someone else in my father's big old house was suddenly appealing. It overrode the common sense telling me not to invite someone back there that I barely knew. The trouble was, and it was odd, but I felt as though I'd known him for ages. I had faith in my ability to judge people as well. My peculiar family had allowed me to hone that skill.

When he insisted on paying for our lunch, I asked if he'd like to come to my house for dinner. I grimaced inwardly. I didn't go around asking men for dates, and it felt awkward.

He agreed with enthusiasm, and the invitation was accepted without any embarrassment.

I'd known for some time I needed to make an effort to make some friends. I told myself this was my first step. I didn't believe it. There were no more plans in my head for any other steps. I wasn't convinced it was a deliberate first step, anyway. It felt reckless, even foolhardy, and I didn't have his number, so I couldn't cancel. To say I was nervous would be an understatement.

With no way of going back on the invitation, I called at Marks and Spencers on my way home to pick up some food and a bottle of wine. They had one of their dinner-for-two offers on, so it didn't cost too much. I found I could afford a first course as well.

He'd been walking into town because parking fees would have been crippling for the number of hours he was spending in the library, but he said he'd drive over that night. He'd raised his eyebrows when I gave him my address.

We lived off Manor Road in one of the old, stone-built houses overlooking the park. I'd never thought about it from anyone else's point of view. It had always been my home, a place my mother ran with efficiency but with selective affection for its inhabitants.

To me though, it was always my father's house, a special building, and I loved it. It had provided me with hidey holes when I was growing up. It had places I could escape to with my books and lose myself for hours. It was also a big place in a desirable area. I could see how it could appear imposing to Jack.

He was exactly on time, but I'd expected this because of his military background. He seemed a little in awe as I let him in. Of course, right then, he didn't know I lived there alone. I guessed he was braced to meet family members. He'd brought flowers, a supermarket bouquet, but very fresh.

"Is everyone out?" he asked, sensing I was alone.

"I live here by myself," I said. I prayed it didn't sound like an open invitation.

He looked at me as if I'd said something unbelievable and then seemed to realise I might think he was being rude. He looked around the spacious hall, taking in the handsome staircase. It was strange to watch him see the house with fresh eyes.

"Do you put your Christmas tree here?" he asked, indicating a space created by the curve in the middle of the staircase. A standard lamp stood there behind an old leather armchair.

What a strange thing to ask. We'd never had a tree there, but then, I couldn't remember the last time we'd bothered with one. I shook my head. All of a sudden, I could see what he meant. It was a space made for an imposing tree.

"A real one, a really tall one, would look brilliant there," he observed, "with loads of lights."

Something of the excited child had emerged from the bulk of his highly trained, solid military frame. As I looked at the space, I could understand what he imagined standing there.

He followed me to the kitchen, where I'd already set the table. The evening was only intended as a meal to be shared by two friends. Using the dining room would be over the top. It would have been a bit chilly in there, too, and I needed to watch the amount of gas I was using. The house was a big, draughty old place, and I needed to be able to pay the bills.

"Show me round," he said, excitement in his voice.

"Why?" I asked.

"Because you live in a real house, and I grew up in a caravan," he said. "It's brilliant."

I was startled, thinking for a moment he might be a traveller, but he laughed and explained how he and his brother had been relegated to the garden as his four sisters grew up and took over the house. I couldn't imagine a family with six children. I was also astonished at his total openness, as the people I knew would never have admitted any hardship in their life.

We did the grand tour of downstairs. He was astonished we had a sitting room, a dining room, a study, and what he called a front room. He liked the study the most, where my father's old polished oak desk sat. Its worn leather top told of the volumes of work he had completed there.

He gazed round, amazed at the number of books crammed into the shelves. They were all there to be used and enjoyed, not for show. Many of them had been the tools of my father's trade. Each one had had its purpose, even in his later years when he was using the internet regularly. There were also the reference books he had written and the books he read for pleasure. He had been an avid reader.

"If this was my house, I'd spend hours in here," he said, gently stroking the wood of the desk. "All these books . . ." His voice trailed off as he surveyed the shelves again.

"My father worked in here a lot. He always looked at home in his chair."

The memory made me smile. My father had loved his captain's chair, and its wood glowed from years of regular use. His fountain pen still lay on the desk, in the exact place it always sat, full of the black permanent ink from the bottle that stood in the top drawer. There were some things I hadn't been able to put away.

There was no way the tour was going to include upstairs. I wasn't stupid. We went back into the kitchen, where the food was ready. I confessed it was really a cheat's meal, but he was impressed as we made our way through the three courses. He settled at one glass of wine because he was driving, and in a strange way, I found it reassuring.

We chatted away, though if I'm truthful, I can't really recall everything we talked about. It's like that when you feel comfortable with someone and the conversation flows. I felt as if the house was glad to have some life in it once again.

"Let's get a Christmas tree at the weekend," he said.

I looked at him in surprise.

"Am I missing something?" I asked.

"You are my girlfriend, aren't you?" He spoke as if he was stating the obvious. "We should get a tree and decorate it together. It'll be fun."

"I didn't realise I was your girlfriend," I replied. My heart pounded as I waited for his reply.

"I sort of assumed you were."

The pounding stopped, and my stomach flipped with joy.

"Have you got decorations and lights?" he asked.

"I suppose there might be some in the attic, but they haven't been out for years. We never had a big tree."

"Then we'll buy new ones," he said. "It's going to look great."

That night, as I lay in bed, I found myself looking forward to getting the tree. I hadn't done anything Christmassy for years. I also thought about his reaction to the house. I loved the old place, but I'd never looked at it the way he'd done. Then again, I'd never had to sleep out in an old caravan for years.

He picked me up early on the Saturday morning and handed me a package. It contained a jolly Christmas jumper, and he chuckled as he opened his jacket to reveal an identical one. I pulled it over the tee-shirt I was wearing, and he looked pleased.

We drove out towards Matlock to pick up a tree and a container. The countryside on the way is always beautiful, but it certainly didn't look Christmassy after all the rain we'd had.

Jack was determined we would have at least a seven-foot

tree, and he was determined it would be symmetrical, straight, and nicely branched from top to bottom. It was glorious to watch the joy it was giving him. It took a good while for him to find the perfect specimen. He didn't flinch at the price and hoisted it on his car roof as if he'd lifted a twig. I left him to it, aware I was starting to feel brighter.

The tree provided a challenge. We had a battle to set it up. It was fun, and I hadn't had much for years. It was a work of art to get the tree vertical and stable in its container. We managed it eventually, despite the gales of laughter as it had lurched, and leaned, and attacked us in all its devious prickly ways.

Exhilarated by our tree victory, we headed to one of the big shops on the retail park. It stocked everything from light bulbs to cuddly unicorns. They had devoted over half of the shop floor to Christmas goods and toys. We filled a barrow with huge plastic tubes of baubles, boxes of lights, and a tree topper. I like a tree with a single colour, two colours at the most, but this was not the year for restraint. Jack wanted a blaze of colour. Since it mattered more to him than me, and he was paying, I was happy to go along.

He added an assortment of other Christmas goods, the cheery sort that had never entered the house before, and the batteries they needed to make them nod, dance, or sing. I added a variety of white candles, suddenly inspired by a vision of log fires and candlelight. I knew there were plenty of logs in the timber shed.

It took a while to pack the car. We had to leave space for our food shopping. He was staying for dinner. I was stunned at what he bought for one meal, but I had never catered for a soldier with a healthy appetite. He had probably left the house hungry the evening he came for dinner.

I'd never had such a glorious afternoon. After we'd put the shopping away, we set about decorating the tree. He found

Christmas music on his phone, and Bing Crosby crooned away in the background as we drowned the seven-foot tree in lights and baubles. It was virtually dark by the time we finished. When he turned the lights on, the tree came to life in a glorious, soaring rainbow of colour.

It seemed corny, but shivers ran down my spine when I saw the magical effect we'd achieved. I couldn't believe a Christmas tree would make me happy. He saw the tears in my eyes, put his muscular arms around me, pulled me into his sturdy chest, and hugged me. He knew I was overcome, and I always like to think he instinctively understood this was the first time I'd seen the house radiating joy. Our first embrace was one of support and concern rather than romance, and I wouldn't have wanted it any other way.

Over dinner we chatted about what we'd be doing on Christmas Day. He was dreading a boozy day in front of the television with his family, and I was not looking forward to a day on my own.

"This is crazy," he said. "I could come over and cook you lunch, and we could spend the day together."

I knew it wasn't an idle offer, because he was a brilliant cook. He had cooked the meal we had just shared, and it had been excellent. I didn't hesitate to accept. It had been a good day, the best I'd spent in a long time, and I wanted more.

"That's settled then," he said. "We'll go food shopping tomorrow."

Jack picked me up the next day, Sunday, and we headed for the supermarket. It was manic in there as everyone was doing their big shops. It took a long time to get round aisles clogged up with families dithering over their choices.

Our trolley filled quickly. It was quite comical, as he was clearly buying in for the sort of Christmas that was pictured in magazines or lived in his imagination.

"I always wanted brandy sauce," he said, tossing a couple of cartons in to go with the pudding we'd already chosen. "We'll need brandy also to flame the pudding. Do you know how to do it?"

I shook my head but reassured him there was brandy in the cupboard at home.

"We'll Google how to do it," he said.

His cheer was infectious, and even the hectic store seemed to have its charms that day. Apparently, we needed champagne, stilton cheese, chocolate mints, and a host of things I'd never have bought. I'd been planning on a small chicken, but Jack insisted on a turkey. I managed to persuade him to buy the smallest one we could find, especially when he threw in a joint of beef. It was clear that we would be spending Boxing Day together, too, and I didn't mind one bit.

"Can you make Yorkshire puddings, or shall we buy frozen? I've never made any."

"I think I can manage to make Yorkshire puddings," I said, "but if we're having beef, I need horseradish sauce."

It was my first and only food request, and he laughed, saying he wasn't sure he could afford my expensive tastes.

The queue to pay was long, but there was plenty to look at and listen to. Slade and Wizard must have collected a fair amount in royalties for the plays of their Christmas songs as we waited. The check-out girls were all wearing novelty hats that twinkled and wobbled as they worked, and for the first time ever, I thought how jolly they looked. I'd have normally thought they were silly.

Jack insisted on paying the bill, which was a relief because even half would have been too pricey for my budget.

We took the shopping home and unpacked. I'd never seen the fridge and shelves as full, even when my mother had thrown one of her dinner parties. She specialised in nouvelle cuisine which meant her portion sizes could—if her guests were honest—be described as mean. I never got to try any left-overs.

We spent the afternoon making mince pies and preparing a trifle. It was amazing how natural it all seemed and how enjoyable it was to work together. I loved the smell of baking, and Jack commented no one baked at his house. Our pies were going to give him his first taste of home-made pastries.

As we worked, I pondered over how I could ask him if he'd like to stay over at Christmas without appearing to be throwing myself at him. I wanted him to be around, but only at the steady pace we were taking.

"You do realise you won't be able to drink much of the wine cellar you just bought if you're driving backwards and forwards?" This was my clumsy attempt to broach the subject.

He'd got the drift, despite my lack of directness. He smiled at me, revealing his slightly crooked teeth. "If you could find a corner for me to curl up in, I suppose I could stay over."

His reply reassured me. There was no misunderstanding there.

"I think we might even find you a whole bedroom," I said, glad he proved we were thinking in the same way.

"Please, don't think you have to invite me to stay over because of all our shopping," he said.

"I don't," I said and gave what I hoped was a reassuring grin.

When he left, I got out fresh linen and made up the bed in Fi's old room. I didn't want him using Charles'. Silly, I know, but Charles' toxicity is pervasive.

I also got logs in ready to get a fire going on Christmas Day in what Jack called the front room. It was the first time that winter I'd lit a fire in there, and I prayed the chimney had been swept at the end of last winter. Knowing my mother's penchant for meticulous planning, I was sure she wouldn't have let me down.

Thinking of her made me think again of how appalled she'd have been over Jack coming to stay. She would have hated the oversized tree and its gaudy decorations. She would have called the battery-operated decorations absolute tat.

"Less is more, Joanna," she would say regularly. "Less is more."

I grinned to myself. It had certainly been true of her portion sizes.

That Christmas, for me at least, it was time for more, and on top of that, even more. Happiness grew inside me.

It was a good feeling.

Marcus made his last trip to the library on Christmas Eve. He wanted to collect as many resources as he could for work he had to do over the holiday. It struck me as sad that he had to get through the next few days on his own, without the wife he had adored.

As there was nothing else for me to do at work that morning, I stayed and chatted for a while.

"Are you going to your brother's for Christmas?" he asked.

I laughed, telling him my only invitation there was to call in for a glass of sherry.

He understood the subtext. "I don't like to think you'll be on your own.

It was thoughtful of him to be concerned, but I was quick to reassure him. "I've invited my friend Jack over. I won't be on my own."

I watched his face fall.

"Is he the chap I've seen you helping out over the last few days?"

When I said it was his expression grew even more concerned.

"Are you sure it's wise? He doesn't look your sort of young

man."

I knew what he meant. Jack's outward appearance wasn't exactly polished.

"He's really nice," I said. "He's very kind, too, and rather old fashioned."

I hoped he could read between the lines and be assured I'd be safe, because I understood and appreciated his concern.

"I was going to say you could come to my house tomorrow if you were at a loose end," he said. "It's not too late, if you want to reconsider."

"That's kind of you, but I'll be totally fine with Jack. Please don't worry."

It was nice of Marcus to be concerned about me. I thought he'd handled it well. He'd checked I wouldn't be on my own and made sure I'd considered my own safety without being rude about Jack.

He rooted in his brief case and took out a present. He looked almost embarrassed as he held it out to me.

"I bought you these," he said. "I hope you like chocolates. I had them gift wrapped at the shop. I'm no good at that sort of thing. I just wanted to thank you for all your help and your excellent work. Happy Christmas."

"Happy Christmas," I leaned forward and lightly kissed both of his cheeks, continental style. "Thank you so much."

He blushed and dismissed the gift as nothing but a small gesture of thanks. He collected up his resources and stashed them away, signalling it was time for him to leave. "Look after yourself, Joanna. You have my number if you need it."

I accepted the words as if they had been spoken by a kindly uncle. It felt good to have someone looking out for me. I watched him leave and then saw Jack. He was running a little late that morning but was sitting at his usual workstation. Apparently, he had been doing some Christmas shopping.

I went over without a thought in my head he would be

concerned about Marcus.

"Who was that?" he asked. "He comes in here a lot."

"Oh, only Marcus. He's a researcher and writer. I do genealogy work for him, and he bought me some chocolates to say thank you."

"Do you always kiss him goodbye?" There was anxiety in his voice and in his features.

"Of course not. He'd bought me a thank you gift. I was just thanking him for it and wishing him a happy Christmas."

"He fancies you."

Fancies. That was a word I'd not heard since I left school, and it made me smile. "Don't be silly."

I'd detected a tinge of jealousy. This was new. I wasn't used to anyone caring enough about me to be jealous.

"He does. I've seen the way he watches you. When you're not looking, he can't keep his eyes off you."

"That's very flattering but totally untrue. He's still mourning the death of his wife."

"If you say so."

He let the matter go and was his usual happy self. I was glad he'd not heard our conversation. I didn't think he'd be pleased if he'd known Marcus had been suspicious of him and protective of me.

Jack

Samantha was curled up on Danny's bed, huddled in her fur jacket against the damp chill of the caravan as I packed my stuff. She is the only member of the family with any common sense and the only one to have any time for me. I think it's because she's the youngest, and Jim and my mam had run out of interest in their brood by the time she was born.

"When will you be back?" she asked. "Will you be here for New Year?"

I didn't know then, but I would never go home again or

spend another night in the caravan. I shrugged my shoulders. I didn't know what my plans were.

"You really like her?" she prompted.

I nodded and handed her the box from my jacket pocket. She fingered the heavy silver locket inside enviously.

"You really like her," she confirmed. "I've never known you interested in a girl before."

She was right. I had been one of the lads since I joined the army, and apart from the occasional overnight entanglement, I'd never been bothered. I couldn't get Jo out of my mind, and it was confusing, scary, and exciting all at the same time.

I handed Samantha an envelope. "Treat yourself," I said awkwardly. I felt bad, having shown her the locket, not to have actually bought her something, but she didn't seem to mind.

She pushed the envelope in her pocket and winked. She knew it was the only gift passing from me to anyone in the house. She uncurled herself, shivering as the chill hit her. She gave me an awkward hug as she left, not because she was uneasy with me, but because our family didn't do hugging. They did sniping and backbiting far more naturally than any show of affection.

I had a lot to think about as I drove over to Jo's. I knew I was trying to give us both a special Christmas time together, and I sensed neither of us had a store of warm memories to draw on for that time of year. I was also really looking forward to spending it in a house where there was space, cigarette smoke-free air, and some warmth from the heating.

How did I feel about Jo? Hard question, because I hadn't known her long. I knew she was special, and I knew she was kind, and she was just about all I'd thought about for a few days. I also knew she was too good for me, but she acted as if she was totally unaware of it. She was really classy.

Had I fallen for the dream of the perfect home, or the girl

who lived there? I was too honest with myself not to face the question and be slightly ashamed to admit I was falling in love with both.

The house looked completely different as I pulled up that night. The tree lights were shining through the windows in the door, and there was a golden flickering coming through the front room window from an open fire. It looked more homely and welcoming than it had seemed before, and I was glad to get inside. I had the strangest feeling of coming home as I looked around the hall again.

The smell of Bolognese sauce and garlic hung in the air, and I was instantly ravenous. Jo had been busy. She showed me upstairs, and I was able to stash my bag.

I couldn't remember ever staying in a bedroom in a house since Danny and I were relegated to the caravan. I must have looked completely stupid as I stared at my new surroundings. Jo broke my train of thoughts by showing me where the landing light switch was and then leading the way to the bathroom.

If I looked stupid in the bedroom, God knows what I looked like in the bathroom. The fittings were all original in a classy sort of way. The clawed feet of the bath still had bits of gilt showing. The toilet bowl was really old and decorated with flowers. Its heavy wooden seat had shiny brass fittings and spoke to me silently of quality. How stupid to be impressed by an old toilet with a cistern on the wall and a hefty chain. Its dainty floral china handle wouldn't have lasted five minutes in our house.

Cleanliness was one of my obsessive traits. I had known what it was like to stink, and the insults from those days still rankled. I stood there breathing in the smells of pine and toilet bleach as if they were some exotic scents.

I must have really lingered in there because when Jo spoke, I started at the sound of her voice.

"I'll go and serve dinner."

She must have thought I was a prat to be so taken by a bathroom.

Have you ever had a perfect evening? I did that night. We sat cross-legged in front of the fire and ate our dinner, accompanied by large glasses of Shiraz. Jo had pulled the curtains and lit candles around the room, and with the heavy door pushed to, that room had a warmth about it I had never known before. A glow of contentment rose inside me, and I was amazed when Jo said that she'd never seen the room looking so cosy.

"It was always a sit still and sit up straight room," she explained. "I had to do a lot of sitting up straight. There was no snuggling in."

Another family uncomfortable with affection, I thought, though we never had to sit up straight. We seemed to have so little in common and yet so much.

"We may be the very first people to sit on this floor to eat their dinner." She laughed.

It had certainly never happened before in her lifetime, and she looked beautiful in the firelight. I'd noticed how pretty she was when working in the library, and it struck me then the best thing of all was she didn't even know it.

There was a shyness about her, and I found it attractive, really attractive. Loading the dishwasher became an ordeal as we had to shimmy up tight as we passed each other. She was close enough for me to smell those lilies of the valley again.

Suddenly, she said she'd finish off by herself. She told me to pour myself another drink and go back to the lounge. I trotted off obediently and contemplated my rising emotions as I sipped the Shiraz. I think she'd had similar feelings to mine.

She soon joined me, but this time she sat beside me and leaned gently against me. We both knew it was her way of telling me it was time to get closer. This was how it had to be. We'd move forward in a way she felt easy with. I had found myself a girl way out of my league, and I didn't want to blow things.

Jo

I stirred on Christmas Day and became aware of sounds from the kitchen. Jack was obviously at work. Not wanting to spoil his surprise, I curled up and thought over the last few days.

Pleased that I'd got Jack's present finished and wrapped, I'd placed it under the tree after he'd gone upstairs the night before. I'd created an album of his family history like those I helped Marcus make and had spent hours at night, after he'd gone home, researching and printing documents, and then assembling them into a coherent story. It proved he and his brother had come from a decent family, which I guessed was what he wanted to know most of all.

With the experience of the commissions I do for Marcus, it had not been as hard as it sounds. He passed the straightforward genealogy jobs to me, and I'm used to pulling them together. It meant I had everything I needed at home to do the research from scratch and create the presentation package. Jack had our premier package waiting for him that morning.

I reflected on the previous evening and smiled to myself. I was pleased. I now knew he'd never had a serious relationship. He'd told me he'd had a few unmemorable brief encounters over the years he'd been in the army.

I'd been honest with him, too. In my first year at university, I'd fallen for a long-haired poet, a literature student who was languishing away, retaking his final year. He had duped me into a relationship. He'd pursued me relentlessly and eventually presented me with a portfolio of love poems he said he'd written for me. I was daft enough to believe him and spent far too long poring over them, trying to find some meaningful lines to cherish and memorise. It had proven difficult.

He wasn't even nice to me. I was disillusioned quickly when a history classmate leaned over to me in a lecture and whispered she'd heard I'd fallen for his poetry scam. I had looked at her in astonishment and then felt utterly stupid. She said it had worked so often the portfolio must be pretty dog-eared. I realised then he'd made me a laughingstock.

Jack was the first person I'd ever shared that shameful story with. I'd always felt naive and stupid about it. He had listened quietly to my sorry tale, but when he heard the rhyming couplet I quoted, the only one I'd found to memorise, he burst into uncontrollable chuckles and laughed until tears trickled from his eyes. For the first time, I could see how utterly stupid it was to feel ashamed, and I laughed until I cried, too.

Between gasps he managed to look at me with what approximated a dopey, poetic gaze, and say, "I would lose my mind if you were unkind."

Perhaps because of the empty bottle of Shiraz, we set off on a new fit of stomach-heaving mirth. It was easy to laugh with Jack.

I was still smiling at the memory when he arrived at my bedroom door bearing a tray with plates of smoked salmon and scrambled eggs and glasses of buck's fizz.

"Breakfast in bed," he said. "Happy Christmas."

Unthinking, I shuffled over to the other side of the bed and threw back the covers to let him join me. He handed me the tray to hold and hopped in beside me.

"Breakfast in bed on Christmas Day with the girl I love," he said breezily and took his plate.

I registered what he'd said with a stupid and childish flutter in my stomach and immediately gave myself a severe warning to proceed with care.

He took his glass and readied it to chink with mine. "Here's to the best Christmas ever."

He was as good as his word. He had meant breakfast in bed quite literally. When we finished, he went to the kitchen with the dishes.

I knew with absolute certainty he was as genuine as he seemed when he opened his present later. It's hard to see a man cry, but tears brimmed in his eyes as he turned the pages. He shook his head in disbelief at what I'd managed to pull together.

"It will take me weeks to read all this," he said.

I took it from him and found the star photograph. I'd tracked it down and got a copy from the local paper. It was dated 1951 and showed Queen Elizabeth accepting a doll house for her granddaughter. It had been commissioned by the town and made by a local carpenter, William Wicks. He was his great grandfather, and there he was, standing next to the queen and looking the image of Jack.

"You've proved it," he said, gratitude shining through his wet eyes. "Danny and me, we're respectable."

Then his irrepressible humour took over. "Well, Danny would be, if he wasn't doing time."

His infectious laugh set me off. It was what I liked best about him. He could make me laugh, and I'd thought I'd forgotten how.

I loved my present. He had snapped a reasonable photograph of me at work when I'd been totally unaware and had paired it with a selfie, allowing us to look at each other across the open locket. I snapped it shut and went to put it on at once. He took it and fastened it round me, nuzzling my neck as he did.

"I meant it earlier," he said. "You're the girl I love. The first girl I've ever loved."

I wanted to believe he meant it, but it wasn't easy to think anyone could fall in love with me as quickly as that.

Charles called round, unannounced, early on the day after Boxing Day. I was still in bed.

Jack was making coffee, and without a thought, he opened the door.

"Who the hell are you?" Charles asked.

I'd heard as I made my way downstairs, "I'm Jack. How can I help you?"

"What the hell is going on, Joanna?" Charles asked as soon as I moved into view.

"Come in." I was irritated, annoyed that he'd shown up out of the blue yet again. Jack looked puzzled. "It's okay. It's my brother." My brother was still waiting for an explanation. "This is Jack. He's staying here for Christmas."

Charles took his time and looked Jack over, deliberately rude in his manner. He took in the close-cropped hair, the tattoos, and the bulging muscles beneath the tight vest. There was a long pause before he spoke. "Taking in strays now you've got the big house to yourself, little sister? Make the most of it while you can. Your days here are limited."

The contempt in his voice was strong, and my face burned with embarrassment. My brother was a cheating, lying snob, and my mother no longer needed to be appeased. There had also been a threat in his words, and I could see Jack had clenched both fists in response. Charles was my problem, not his. I handled it.

"Jack's a soldier," I said, as if that explained everything. I'd made my voice as sweet as I could. I sensed Jack straightening to his full height. "I'm doing Help for Heroes this Christmas. Anyway, what did you want?"

Charles' bravado disappeared, and it had everything to do with Jack's menacing frame behind me.

"We're entertaining today, and Amanda has sent me for the canteen of cutlery."

I had let Charles and Amanda take anything they wanted when I took over the house, and I had always been surprised they'd left that. The canteen had always stood in its mahogany box on the dining room sideboard in plain sight. It housed twelve complete place settings in hallmarked silver and came from our mother's family.

"Take it," I said. I didn't want it, but it clearly mattered to my brother. "Anything else while you're here?"

Charles had no ear for irony. "Are those tureens still in the pantry? The ones with lids?"

"Help yourself," I said, having no interest in them.

I could see Jack was getting angrier. I didn't want a scene over things I didn't care about, but it did feel good to have someone on my side. I was relieved when Charles had gotten together the things he wanted, and I was surprised when Jack helped him load it all into the car. I stood at the door and watched.

Jack closed the car's rear door with a smile and then grasped the collar of Charles' Barbour jacket, pulling him round so they were eye-to-eye.

"Don't just turn up here again," he said. "Phone first. Make sure it's convenient."

I'm almost certain I hear him conclude with *capiche?* and that made me smile. Anyway, *capiche* or not, he'd convinced my brother he meant what he said. Charles scrambled into the car and took off rapidly. I admit I really enjoyed that.

"What was all that about?" Jack asked. "Does he just turn up and help himself?"

"Let's have coffee, and I'll tell you all about it."

Jack listened to the complex story of my family and our inheritance without interrupting. There was a pause as he had a lot to take in. Eventually, he said he'd make toast and, as he was going through the door, he said with a grin, "Help for Heroes. Brilliant!" and we both laughed.

We sat on the rug in front of the fire he'd lit in the lounge and ate our toast.

"So, he owns a third of this house?" I nodded. "He owes you and your sister 50k each?" I nodded again. "He can't pay you unless the house is sold, and he can't sell the house because you own over half of it?"

He bit his toast thoughtfully.

"I can't sell without his agreement," I clarified. "Not that I want to."

We'd come a long way in our relationship in the last two days, and I'd now taken a risk to share all this information.

"If you buy him out, you could own this place yourself?" I nodded. "Then why not do it and get rid of him for good?"

It sounded so simple, but I knew that Charles would be as awkward as he could. I'd not had the stomach for the fight. I tried to explain it all and was aware I sounded scared of my brother, which I wasn't, but something was worrying me about him that I couldn't quite make out. He'd lost weight and he wasn't looking as confident as he usually did. I pushed it out of my mind and went on with my tale.

"I'm not ready for a battle with my brother. My feelings are still too raw after losing my parents. I'm not strong enough to get into a fight with him."

"You have to stand up to him. He thinks he can bully you."

"That's because he always has done."

"You're not facing him alone now. I won't let him walk all over you. We can face him together and sort it out."

I looked at him, and I could see he meant it. It had sounded simple when I heard Jack say it, but I wasn't sure what he meant by facing him together. I wasn't even sure we were going to be together beyond those few days.

"Well, there's nothing I can do until after New Year. Everywhere is closed." I was being deliberately evasive.

"How much would it take to buy him out?"

Jack was not going to let this go.

"The house is worth three hundred and sixty-thousand pounds." I knew because it had been valued for probate. "He'd need one hundred and twenty thousand from me, and he'd have to pay fifty thousand back to me and Fi each. That would only leave him with twenty thousand. He'd never go for it. He thought when our mother died, he'd get the house to himself and the debt wiped off. He's got a lot of resentment and greed over not getting his way."

"Some brother!" he said. "We'll sort something out. We'll work out a deal he can't refuse."

Jack

I remembered how I'd lain awake in bed for ages on Christmas Eve, just taking in my surroundings. I was actually counting my blessings. There I was in a real bed in a big, warm bedroom. The pillows were soft and comfy. The duvet cover smelt of flowers. I guessed that was what fabric conditioner did, because my laundry never smelled anything like it. I'd been in hotel beds, but this was different. It was in a house. It made me realise how much me and Danny had missed out on. Clean sheets didn't happen very often at our house.

Things had changed since then. Charlie Boy had visited, and I had a lot on my mind. I'd hated her rat-faced brother on sight. He had messed things up for me. One minute I was finding myself falling in love with the girl from the library and taking things nice and steady. For God's sake, we'd only got as far as kissing. We'd just had the best Christmas I can remember. I'd spent it as her welcome guest in her lovely home. I'd been looking forward to us taking things slowly and seeing where they went. I didn't want to scare her off.

After his visit, my mind was working overtime to figure out how we could buy rat-face out and live together happily ever after. Was it a knight in shining armour response? I wasn't sure. He'd made me so mad I wanted to show him I was no stray and wasn't scared of him. Was I just hitting back at his smugness?

Was it anger, fate, love, or just me being a chancer? I had just a dozen days of leave left, and it all felt a bit too much. Just then Jo came into the room carrying a tray of coffee and mince pies, looking as classy and well-groomed as ever. I knew then it was love. She was not only the girl of my dreams. She was the girl beyond my dreams. She wasn't just a damsel in distress. She really mattered to me.

She had been instinctively taking care of me, something no one had ever done. Simple things like making me a coffee, putting my washing through the machine, and making sure I had fresh towels. She'd shown me more consideration than I'd ever known. Danny had always looked out for us and nicked stuff to keep us going, but he didn't do those sorts of things.

Could I imagine being without her? I knew the answer was no.

"What's wrong?" she asked, sensing I was staring.

"I was just thinking how much I love you," I replied. "Wondering what we should do about it."

She sat down beside me and looked at me in the searching way she had, as if weighing up if she could believe me. "Do we have to do anything about it?" she asked. "Isn't it just about how things are and seeing how they go?"

She wasn't saying she loved me. "Well, I think we do. This is real. It's come out of the blue, and we need to grab it with both hands," I knew I was talking too fast and coming out with cliches, but I wasn't good with words. It was the best I could do.

"What do you want us to do?"

"Get married, buy your brother out of this house, make it

our home, and have babies. Boys, if we can, but girls will do."

She looked stunned, amused, and pleased, all at the same time.

"Your timescale for all this?" she asked with eyebrows raised.

"Well, I've nothing planned for this week, so we could get married before I go back to camp."

"Drink your coffee," she said. "That's a lot to take in."

Jo

It was more than a lot to take in. It was a lifechanging set of proposals.

I'd once had my life planned out. At school, I'd known what subjects to take, what university I was aiming for, what grades I needed to get on the course I wanted. Of course, things had derailed slightly when I'd come home to look after my father. I'd ended up with a second-class degree and not a first. I hadn't been able to stay on to do my Master's and PhD. It meant I'd need to find another university, a less prestigious one, and it had cut me deeply.

I'd not gone back to my studies for the stupidest, stubbornest reason. I'd ended up with two thirds of the house I loved, and because of not being ready to give up my father's house, I'd got myself a job at the library and stayed on. I hadn't wanted to leave it and exchange it for student digs. I also discovered irritating Charles was satisfying, after all he'd done to try to boost his inheritance.

"Let's go for a drive and a long walk," I said. "I'm still thinking."

It was as damp as ever and chilly, but we wrapped up and drove along the A6, heading towards Matlock Bath. That drive was always uplifting, and the walks at the end were always good. I wanted to work some things out as we tramped along. It was slippery as we walked up the Heights of

Abraham, but at least we were in fresh air.

He knew I needed to be left to my own thoughts. He just put his arm around me, drew me to him, and we walked in silence.

I liked having his arm around me, I liked being nestled against his strong frame and feeling his warmth, and I became increasingly aware I was happy.

It came as a surprise to me. I couldn't remember the last time it had happened, but I was happy right then. I was feeling light and skippy inside, like I'd done when I was young, and it was going to be my birthday. I was in love, and it felt right. I was sure things would work out in a way they'd never done on my birthday. Birthdays had always ended up with my mother having one of her please-be-quiet-and go-to-your-room-headaches. Jack was not going to treat me as she had, and I knew it after just a few days.

I'm sure Jack was feeling the same strong emotions, because he stopped, pulled me round to face him, and kissed me with passion in a way we hadn't kissed before. We broke away, both a little breathless, looked at each other, and we knew. This was good. It was real. It was for ever.

"We'd better get back," he said, looking at the darkening sky. "Now you've done your thinking."

I nodded. I had decided to marry him and make my life with him. Right then, it felt like the best decision I'd ever made. He knew. That was how it was going to be with us. We would always know what the other was thinking.

I'd met my soulmate.

The atmosphere in the car was charged as we drove home. There was an electricity between us I had never felt before, and all I knew was we had to make love.

The ever-changing speed restrictions on the A6 were not helping us get home as fast as we would have liked. Both of us sighed heavily a few times as the heavy traffic obediently slowed time and time again, and we had to follow suit.

I'd never felt anything like it before. It had taken me completely by surprise. When we got back home, Jack turned and held out his hand as he started to climb the stairs. I took it willingly.

We discovered a part of our lives that afternoon that was both primeval and tender. We had embarked on something that was as essential to us as the food we shared or the breaths we took. It was precious, exquisite and to us, sacred. It was our private world, and to speak of it would desecrate it.

Curled up together, exhilarated and content, we looked ahead. We agreed if we accepted being together was our only priority, we could work everything else out. I had absolutely no doubts this man wanted to bind his life to mine forever.

Jack had the mind of a soldier, and he could reduce the tangle of decisions lying ahead of us into a logical sequence of actions. When he went through them that afternoon, they all seemed perfectly achievable. I listened, astonished at how perceptive he was in creating an overview.

We added details, deciding we would make arrangements the next day to marry before Jack had to return to Catterick. We became distracted again, as we would many times more. We were soulmates and lovers, and we both knew we could work everything out together.

Sorting the house out had to be led by me—two-thirds of it was already in my name. The first thing I did was to telephone Thomas West. I knew it wasn't fair to ring him at that time of year, when his firm was closed, but I couldn't wait.

He was as charming as ever and invited us over to his house the next afternoon. He lived at Ashbourne, but I'd never visited him there. Jack was as sure as ever in knowing the way without any help from me. It was as if he had GPS hard wired into his brain. He was less sure about what Thomas would make of him, but I had faith. Thomas was no fool. He could see through my brother.

We were both shocked when we pulled into the drive entrance. The man lived in a mansion. Of course, I knew he'd have money, but this place was beyond all expectations. I could sense Jack tensing as we waited for the door to open.

Thomas West was nothing like my brother. If he didn't like the look of Jack, his good manners didn't let him show it. He took us into the drawing room and offered us tea, but we were both too nervous to accept.

He already knew we were seeking his advice about buying Charles out because of my phone call. I explained that we were getting married and that we'd been that morning to arrange a civil ceremony for Saturday. All we had to do was to wait for the paperwork to arrive that would allow the wedding to go ahead.

Thomas West slowly arranged his fingertips together, so they were touching. I'd seen him do that many times before when he was thinking something through. We waited like naughty children, sitting before their headteacher and the silence was unnerving. Then he lowered his hands and spoke.

"Talk me through the finances," he said.

I started with the valuation from probate, reminded him of the debt Charles owed to Fi and me, and ended with my fear that Charles would never agree to accept the market value and wouldn't sell his share.

"Yes," he said, almost impatiently. "How do you propose to buy him out?"

Jack understood more quickly than I had that Thomas West was looking out for me. He took a notebook from his pocket and opened it to the right page before offering it to Thomas.

"Those are my savings." He pointed to a row of figures. "You can see the total, and that is my annual salary below."

He paused to let the elderly solicitor absorb them.

"I wouldn't want to use all my savings, but I should be able to get a mortgage to cover the shortfall. If I provide the funds to buy Jo's brother out, it will feel like it's all right for me to live there."

Thomas looked at Jack, his eyes boring into him. It struck me how he was reassessing his initial judgment, but I couldn't be sure. He always had an inscrutable manner when it came to business. He pored over the figures, and I knew he'd be surprised at how strong Jack's finances were. I'd been amazed when he showed me the numbers.

"As you know, I'm your father's executor," Thomas said to me. "You can maintain occupancy of the house until there is a change in your circumstances, at which time the house must be sold. Your marriage, in my opinion, would constitute that change."

My heart was racing, and I knew Jack was getting nervous. Did he mean we couldn't just buy Charles out? Did Thomas mean to insist the house was sold on the open market?

"You're going to have to leave this with me. I shall have to get in touch with Charles' solicitor."

"Can't we just buy him out?" I asked.

"Well, I see no advantage in putting the house on the market and incurring agents' fees and costs, do you? I shall explain all that to his solicitor. However, I'd like you to get three new valuations for me as soon as you can, and if Charles wants independent valuations, you will have to allow it. To be honest, I'm sure your brother will want to secure the highest possible."

He paused again. "I would like you to get a full survey done on the house. It will be expensive, but I see your fiancé will be able to cover that. It's in your interests to know the faults in the property and to reflect them in the final price you're prepared to pay."

Suddenly, I understood what he was saying. A survey should counter any inflated valuation Charles might obtain.

"Oh, and one more thing," he said, "I've already received my fees for handling your father's estate. There will be no further charges."

Jack stood and stretched out his hand. "Thank you, sir," he said, shaking Thomas' hand in gratitude.

"By the way, if you have any difficulty getting the paperwork through to allow you to marry on Saturday, contact me. I might be able to help."

"Thank you," we said in unison.

We were both overcome with gratitude, and I knew that the reason he was being kind was because of the old bond he'd had with my father. He had assessed Jack during that interview and had approved of him.

He called to his wife, and she came in, an elegant and stylish woman who I guessed to be in her early seventies.

"My dear, Joanna is going to marry this young man on Saturday," he said.

"Congratulations," she said. "I'm pleased for you." She kissed us both as if we were dear friends, although I had only seen her a couple of times in my life.

"Do you have your dress?" she asked.

"I'm going to find something in my wardrobe," I replied.

"Nonsense," she said. "Get your young man to drop you off here at ten on Thursday. You and I, my dear, are going shopping, and Thomas will be paying."

I must have looked stunned, and Thomas realised I didn't know how to respond.

"Your father was my dearest friend, and I promised him I would look after you. Let us do this for you," he said. "We'd discussed it after you called, but it all depended on Jack, here." He clapped an approving hand on Jack's shoulder.

"I passed, then," Jack said.

"Only just," Thomas said with a beam.

Chapter Four

Jack

I was walking into town. I'd told Jo I wanted to do a bit of shopping and would only be an hour or so. My mind was spinning. I couldn't believe everything had worked out. We'd been to a genuine manor house to get advice. I'd been right to suspect a lot rested on whether Thomas West believed in me. Thank God, he did. He liked me. Me, Jack, the boy who was dragged up by his brother, who had only been a kid himself at the time.

Jo was a lot more settled now about the house. Our visit to Thomas West had given her hope. She'd been scared we faced a long battle with her brother with little chance of success.

We had been thrown into a frenzy of phone calls. As we suspected, most places were shut for the holidays, and those that were open had no staff to come out and do valuations until after New Year. We made appointments with them and found a surveyor who could visit on the second of January.

I got in touch with camp and was able to arrange marriage leave. I would have another fortnight with Jo after the wedding, which meant I'd be there for their visits.

This wasn't like my life. My life consisted of the army, my mates, and Danny, and it had been enough. Now there was Jo, and a wedding, and a house. I'd never allowed myself to even dream of such a life.

We even got the call to say the wedding could go ahead on Saturday as we planned, and we'd been to buy wedding rings. My Jo is adorable, not like the women my army mates married. They always wanted the biggest and flashiest thing they could screw out of my mates.

She wouldn't look at fancy or flashy rings. She knew exactly what she wanted. A plain, slim gold wedding band that felt smooth on her finger. She wouldn't look at engagement rings because we had a house to buy. She wasn't interested in fancy rings, she said, she just wanted to marry me.

It made me realise once again how she'd never fit in with camp life. She'd have so little in common with the women she'd meet. Being married to me, she wouldn't be mixing with the officers' wives. We'd totally dismissed the idea of married quarters at Catterick. We both wanted to make her father's house our home. We were doing the right thing in buying the house, and it wasn't a case of me taking advantage.

I didn't even know how much longer I'd stay in the army now things had changed so much. I wanted to finish the degree course the army was putting me through. I'd have been crazy not to, but afterwards, I could imagine a life outside the army with Jo and our kids. I didn't want to delay being together for too long.

Our kids would have a mam and dad who loved them and a home they could be happy in. I'd not had dreams like this before. I did then, and I wasn't going to mess up.

I'd walked quickly and was at the jewellers in no time. It was where we'd bought our wedding rings. My mind had been churning things over since I left the house. I needed to concentrate because I was going to get Jo an engagement ring. I knew exactly what she'd want because of her reaction to the flashy ones. I already knew her size. Within five minutes I was leaving the shop, ring in my pocket. The jeweller said it was the fastest engagement ring purchase he could remember.

I headed home to get engaged appropriately. It was daft, but getting engaged really mattered to me. I'd overridden Jo's decision not to have a ring because I wanted to do things right. I didn't want people looking down on me. I had a ten-minute walk in front of me, less if I rushed, and then I'd get down on one knee and propose properly.

Jo

Jack had gone shopping, but he said he'd only be an hour. I thought I'd use the time to prepare the dinner and tackle the ironing. No matter how exciting life was just then, there was no escaping the basics. He'd only been gone a few minutes when the bell rang. I reminded myself yet again I needed to get keys cut for him. I guessed he'd forgotten something.

It wasn't Jack. It was Charles. I'd never seen him so wild. He barged in past me. I closed the door and followed him.

"I know you're on your own," he said. "I waited until I saw him go out."

It sounded menacing, and I felt uneasy. This was not a Charles I'd ever known or seen before. He didn't even look like my dapper brother. He was wearing a hoodie, a baseball cap, and trainers. Charles never dressed like that. He was agitated. He was talking too fast, and was twitchy, as if he was on something.

"I thought I'd pay you one last visit."

It sounded ominous. He'd always been spiteful, but he'd never hurt me. I took confidence from that and breathed deeply as he paced through the house. He was moving quickly, going from one room to another. He repeated the same circuit over and over. It was maniacal. Its frenzy scared me, seeming to have been going on for hours. My panic increased, making my heart thud against my chest.

Eventually his pacing stopped. He stayed completely still for a few minutes. I think he was searching for words in his fevered brain.

"This should all have been mine," he said, breaking the oppressive silence. "Fi didn't want anything to do with this miserable house. If it wasn't for you, she'd have signed it over to me. It's all your fault."

My stomach tightened. This felt threatening. I didn't know how to respond. I wasn't going to tell him Fi would have set fire to the house rather than sign it over to him.

"I told you years ago you should never have been born. Ma should have got rid of you. You ruined her life, and now you're ruining mine. She always wished you were dead."

That hit me hard. Had my mother said that?

"If you hadn't poisoned Pa against me, he'd have never wanted that money back. He'd have looked after his son, like a decent father should."

By then he was agitated again. He bolted upstairs. I followed him, finding him in our parents' room. He seemed surprised it was untouched. I suppose he thought I would have moved in.

"I'm still in my room," I said. "Your room is just as you left it." I hoped it would sound reassuring. I wanted to make him feel better.

He went into his old room and looked around. Nothing had changed since the day he left. "Stinking hole," he said, slamming the door on the way out so hard it rattled in its frame.

The noise echoed across the landing. He rushed down the stairs and I followed, filled with apprehension.

"Can I make you a drink?" It sounded pathetic, but I couldn't think of anything else to say. I wanted to restore some sort of normality.

"I don't want a fucking drink. I want this house and all that's in it. I want the money you stole from me. That's why I'm here. Have you any idea what you've done to me?"

I shook my head.

"You've ruined me. I'm done. I'm finished." He pushed his face into mine. The smell of his breath made me pull my head away. "Don't you back away from me. You know what you've done. Now it's payback time."

He grabbed my hair, twisted it, and threw me into the armchair by the fire. "I hope, dear sister, you enjoyed your victory while it lasted. We are going to finish this nonsense right now. It all ends here," he said. "This house is mine and always has been."

Even though I was seated, he gave me a shove, and I hit the chair cushions with some force.

I wasn't sure what he meant by ending it, but I was scared. My heart was beating hard, the pounding was not just in my chest. It was also in my throat, choking me, and in my ears, deafening me. He'd always hated me, but he'd never put a hand on me before.

"You think you're oh so superior with your university degree, but I'm the clever one. I'm not here, see. I'm in Birmingham on a course. I'm all registered, and my car is still there. I slipped out, got changed, came up on the train, and will be back on the train in one hour. You'll be dead before anyone has missed me."

Pre-meditated and sinister, it was surreal, yet brutally real at the same time.

"I'm your next of kin," he said. "With you gone, I own the whole lot. No need for lawyers. I shall grieve, of course, just long enough to get the paperwork all sorted."

He wanted to kill me. My brother, the one who had wanted me aborted all those years ago, wanted to kill me. The Charles I knew was a bully and a coward, and all I could hope then was he wouldn't have the guts to do it.

"What are you going to do?"

He pulled a piece of tightly braided blue cord from his

pocket and wound it round both hands to display a length sufficient to go round my neck. "I'm afraid I'll have to make it look as though you've been sexually assaulted so no one suspects me, but I'll wait until you're dead." He sneered. "I wouldn't want to embarrass you."

He looked at the cord with sinister delight and lunged, forcing it round my neck. Coarse, it chafed my skin as he dragged it round, and it scratched my fingers as I fought to get them underneath it to ease the pressure. He pulled me off the armchair with it, choking me as I fell.

I struggled to break free, and it startled him. I don't think he'd prepared himself for a fight when he concocted his plan. As he fought to manage my writhing body, he knew I was going to resist with all my strength.

"You're just my pathetic little sister."

He leaned over me, pressing me down with his full weight, increasing the tension on the cord. I was fighting to breathe, and I knew I had to do something more.

I drew my knee up sharply into his groin with such force he lurched back, fell to his side, and folded over, groaning in pain. I guess he'd never been kneed in the testicles before.

I heaved myself up and grabbed the poker from the hearth. I could have brought it down on his head then, as he was doubled in agony, but just as I believed Charles was no killer, neither was I.

He looked up and saw me with the poker aloft, and lunged at me, grabbing my wrist. Twisting to jerk free of him, I lost my grip on the poker and its fancy handle cracked my forehead as it fell to the ground. We both crashed to the floor. The force of the fall threw me backwards. My head struck the raised hearth with a thud, leaving it propped up awkwardly on the cold marble. My eyes closed with sickening pain sweeping through my head. When I opened them, Charles was leaning over me. The cord was still around my neck, but he wasn't tightening it anymore.

He was howling with his head thrown back.

He must have thought the blow had already killed me. I played dead, closing my eyes again before he looked back at me. It's hard to feign death and to breathe without the chest rising and falling, but I did my best. Warm blood trickled down my face, and I could smell its ferrous tang. I realised the blow from the poker must have cut my head open. Raving and out of his mind at the sight of all the blood, he didn't pay attention to my vital signs.

"Oh, my God," he groaned again and again.

All I could do was maintain my deathly position and repress my breathing. The seconds, feeling like hours, ticked away. It grew harder and harder to maintain the pretence of death as the blood ran down my face and trickled into my mouth. The clarity I had astounded me as I listened to Charles' groaning. The front door opened. It was Jack. He must have picked up my keys after all. Right then, that stupid detail seemed amazing and miraculous. I opened my eyes.

"Jo," Jack called and came into the room.

He absorbed the scene in a second, showing his military training immediately. He grabbed Charles and dragged him away from me. He punched him hard enough to make his head snap backwards and flung him across the room. Charles crashed against the sideboard and our mother's beloved knickknacks, the ones he'd mockingly rejected, tumbled down on his head.

I was in Jack's arms, and Charles was no further threat.

"Call an ambulance," I said.

"The police," Jack replied.

"An ambulance and get me a towel."

Charles was sobbing now. I shrugged myself free of Jack's arms and half-crawled to my brother. I put my arms around him and held him, and he howled against my shoulder.

"You're mad," Jack said. "He tried to kill you."

"An ambulance and a towel," I said, aware I was dripping blood on Charles' hoodie as I rocked him gently. "I think my brother has had a breakdown."

The cut on my head had stopped bleeding by the time the ambulance crew arrived, but I still looked a blood-stained mess. I was holding my brother in my arms, still rocking him gently.

I told them what I wanted them to know. I left out the attempted murder and told them my brother had had a violent episode. I'd told Jack what had happened whilst we waited, and there was no way he was going to keep quiet.

Jack told them what he wanted them to know. "He tried to murder her," he said. He was seething. "He'd got his alibi sorted. He was even going to sexually assault her after she was dead and then head back to Birmingham and re-join his course as if nothing had happened. He'd planned it all."

The crew could see Charles was traumatised and shaken. Jack had told them how he'd dragged him off me and punched him. They checked him over thoroughly, then checked me too. They assured me the wound was small and the bleeding had stopped. They applied steri-strips to make sure. They wanted me to go in hospital for observation in case of concussion, but I was convinced I'd never lost consciousness and refused to go.

Jack wanted me to go and offered to drive me, since it was clear I couldn't share an ambulance with Charles. I was determined I wasn't going, and all they could do was give me the advice I was expecting. I was to go to A and E immediately if any sickness, severe headache, or blurred vision came on. I'm ashamed to say, I stopped listening. Jack didn't. He repeated the indicators slowly and carefully, committing them to his memory.

The crew leader turned to me, irritated by my attitude, and said, "I don't know what's gone off here, love. I don't want to, but we will be reporting it to the police. I expect you'll be hearing from them soon."

Charles was oblivious to everything going on around him. Jack and I followed them and watched them load him into the ambulance and drive away.

"Thank God for that," Jack said, and we went indoors.

"Hold me," was all I had to say, and to his credit, he did. He kept his thoughts to himself for as long as I stayed clinging to him, whimpering into his sleeve.

CHAPTER FIVE

Jack

That dream existence of mine didn't last long. After all that, the night was not going to turn into the celebration I planned. The engagement ring stayed in my jacket pocket whilst we got ourselves sorted. Jo was my priority. I ran a bath and encouraged her to soak a while, and I helped her wash the dried blood off her skin and out of her hair. As angry as I was with her brother, I was desperate to take care of her.

She came down in her dressing gown and curled up on the sofa. When she leaned on me, as always happened, the faint scent of lily of the valley drifted from her.

"This is all my fault," I said. "I'm sorry. If we hadn't looked into buying him out of the house, he wouldn't have gone crazy."

I didn't tell her I'd put her at risk by going against her wishes. I'd left her alone to get her the ring she'd said she didn't want. Above all, I was blazing mad because she didn't want to prosecute him. The poisonous piece of dirt would get away with it, and I didn't want her to see I wanted him to pay big time for all he'd done to her.

Jo sighed. "When we're married, you'll be my next of kin, and he can go to hell. Roll on Saturday."

I knew she had a point. What a night. We'd no sooner gotten settled when the police came, and we had to go through it all again. We found out Charles was in hospital, awaiting a psych assessment and was under sedation.

I give Jo credit. She told them exactly what had happened. She didn't sugar-coat it, but she was determined they understood her brother was ill and not responsible for what he'd done. She said he'd been behaving irrationally for some time and must have become delusional, because he would never be able to kill anyone.

"Does your brother have money troubles?" was one of the questions they asked.

Up until then, I'd assumed his motive to be greed, wanting what Jo had inherited. Her next statement took me by surprise. Jo was never nasty about anyone. It was not like her to be critical.

"My brother always has money troubles. His wife has expensive tastes."

They took my statement, too. I didn't mess about. I told them I'd come in and seen him leaning over Jo, who was lying still and covered in blood, how I'd dragged him off her and punched him. If it meant I was guilty of assault, then it was just too bad. I told them I'd do the same thing again if anyone hurt her.

They took their time, and when they left, I got Thomas West's number and called him. The biggest surprise there was to hear he'd not been able to contact Charles' solicitor. This meant Charles knew nothing of me and Jo wanting to buy his share of the house. The guy really must have money troubles to have dreamt up his crazy scheme.

I was relieved to hear it. It meant I hadn't brought all this trouble down on Jo, who was getting tired of telling me not to feel guilty. She was also fed up with me asking her if she was okay, but I was scared. I knew all about blows to the head from army training.

"Let's go to bed," she said. "I'm going shopping for my wedding dress tomorrow. I will need some energy."

She managed a smile, and I thought of the ring. Why not?

Some good had to come out of today. I took the ring box out of my coat pocket as I followed her into the hall.

It was not the night for a big romantic scene. I simply told her I loved her and wanted her to have my ring. She was glad to end the day with something good, and she went to sleep wearing it. I curled round her like a protective guard dog, taking in the faint scent of lilies as I listened to her steady breathing.

No way I'd be going to sleep that night. I had to watch over my girl.

Jo

I woke up, and the first thing I did was check that my ring was still on my finger. It was amazing that had been my first thought after all that had happened. I needed to get rid of all the horror and focus on Jack.

The excitement about our wedding was there, churning away in my tummy. It was Thursday, and Mrs. West and I were going shopping for my dress. It was lovely to have someone to share that with, and Mrs. West seemed nice.

I rolled over. In what light was coming in from the landing, I saw Jack. He was watching me from the big armchair in the corner, smiling.

"How long have you been there?"

"Hours," he said. He slipped in beside me and put his arms round me. "You smile a lot when you're asleep."

"That's because I was dreaming about my ring," I replied. "It was good for something nice to happen yesterday."

He embarked on his round of questions. Did I have a headache? Was my eyesight clear? Did I feel sick? Irritating though his fussing was, it was a new and comforting feeling that someone really cared. I wanted more of that. I watched him pad away to fetch tea and toast and thanked the heavens for finding me this man.

I wondered how Charles was and whether the police would charge him. I had made it quite clear that I wouldn't press charges. I realised he must be in a real mess financially, and I knew it was because he couldn't say no to Amanda. Their house had been fiendishly expensive and was exquisitely furnished. The boys were at private school, and the whole family were health club and tennis club members. Amanda and Charles were also leading lights in the city's most exclusive golf club. All that took paying for.

I knew the property market was buoyant with continuously low interest rates, meaning Charles' turnover from his estate agency should be healthy. Was it healthy enough to pay for all that and their trips abroad? I doubted it. They'd been glad enough to manoeuvre our mother into paying for their last holiday.

I reached for my mobile and called the hospital. I got through to the right place eventually and, of course, they asked what my relationship was to Charles. When I told them I was his sister, they apologised but said his wife had expressly told them to give me no information whatsoever.

I was still reeling with shock when Jack arrived with the tea and toast. Charles had come here intending to kill me, I'd not pressed charges, and my sister-in-law had banned me from knowing how he was.

Jack was furious, and I knew that, once again, he regretted my decision to let things lie. He phoned Thomas West again, and they had a long conversation about what had happened. It did him good to talk things over with someone with a clinical detachment. Although Thomas was totally appalled by what had happened, he could still analyse the situation professionally.

Jack did his best to explain I thought Charles had had a total breakdown and had not been responsible for his actions the previous day. Thomas offered to talk my options through with me, but I declined. My mind was made up.

Shortly afterwards his wife called to see if I was well enough to go with her for my dress. I sighed. Charles was not going to spoil my day. I wouldn't let him. I was definitely going shopping for my wedding dress. I couldn't wait to be Jack's wife. I thanked her for her concern but assured her I would be there on time.

Getting married was what was important, and when I said that to Jack his face broke out into a beaming smile.

"You're right," he said, "and whilst you two are shopping, I will get myself a suit." He laughed his deep, hearty laugh. "I'll need one now I'm going up in the world. Leroy's in jail, I can't borrow his."

I'm naturally reserved and shy with people I don't know very well, but Mrs. West had a way of being able to put me at ease. She insisted I call her Lydia, and it felt comfortable. She was anxious about the events of the previous day and reassured herself I was well enough to go out with her. She brushed back my hair in a motherly way to inspect my wound.

"You got away lightly, all things considered," she said. "It must have been an ordeal."

"Getting married to Jack puts it into perspective," I replied. "That's the future, and I've consigned my brother to the past."

"Very wise," she agreed, though I sensed she thought I was being overly confident about my ability to put everything behind me.

She was a woman with connections across the county, and it came as no surprise that she was a good friend of the owner of an exclusive bridal shop. She'd made an appointment for us, and she seemed as girlishly excited as I was to step into the chandeliered opulence of her friend's shop.

Her friend, Dee, listened to what I had in mind and nodded as if she understood exactly. She reappeared with three dresses over her arm, threw open the curtain to the changing room, and hung them on the rail.

Even as they hung there in their protective polythene, I knew she had understood. Not a frill or flounce in sight, just simple, ivory dresses that were already transmitting their elegant simplicity to me through the polythene.

I glanced at the ticket on the nearest one and shook my head immediately. Elegance and simplicity obviously came at a high price, far too high to expect the Wests to pay.

Dee, however, shook her head and smiled. "There's a special price for Lydia."

She pulled the curtain behind us and busied herself unwrapping the dresses whilst I slipped off my jeans and sweater. "Which one first?"

One had captured my attention from the minute I'd seen it. I was surprised at how heavy it was as she helped me into it, but once it lay on my shoulders, it felt weightless. I looked in the mirror and saw what I'd hoped to see, a fitted top cut in a way that it hid the sores around my neck. It must be pretty unusual to have to choose a wedding dress to hide strangulation marks, but thankfully Dee didn't mention them.

The dress had a gently flaring skirt that just crumpled slightly on the floor, but I wasn't wearing shoes. I loved it.

Dee opened the curtains to let Lydia see. She didn't need to say anything. I could tell by her face she was getting quite emotional when she saw me in the dress. I tried the other two on and, although they were beautiful dresses, they didn't seem to belong to me the way the first one had. Lydia and Dee rejected them both on sight.

Dee found me a pair of satin shoes to lift the hemline to the right length and a neat pearl headband which slipped into the natural shaping of my hair and let my fringe fall to cover my wound. I looked at myself in the mirror. I still looked like me, but I looked like a bride. I also looked happy, which was amazing after the events of the previous day.

It was such an odd feeling to see my reflection. I don't think I will ever own anything more perfect than my wedding dress, and the feel of it on my body told me why it was expensive.

I was enchanted. Lydia was delighted and didn't flinch at the final bill, which they hid from me. Whilst I got changed, Dee produced a chilled bottle of Prosecco, three flutes, and poured us a celebratory drink. It was all so deliciously frivolous and joyful I found my eyes filling with tears when I joined them and saw how happy they were for me.

It was the perfect antidote to the horrors of the day before.

For the wedding, we had only one witness each. Jack had asked his sister to act as a witness, and I had asked Marcus Burrows. Jack had sworn his sister to absolute secrecy about our marriage. He didn't want anyone else from his family there. To be fair, she didn't need convincing.

He wasn't keen on my choice, still clinging on to the idea that Marcus had designs on me. However, Brenda and her family always decamped to Blackpool for Christmas and the New Year, making her unavailable. She would have been my number one choice, but I was still happy to ask Marcus.

"Are you sure about this, Joanna?" he'd asked. "You hardly know him. It seems very quick to me, and you're from different worlds."

I appreciated his honesty, and I knew he was only saying what Brenda would have said. I was able to reply with confidence. "I've never been so sure."

"I'll do this because I will always support you, but I advise you to take a step back and think." he said. "Live together, give yourself time to make a prenup. This all seems too quick. You could always marry him in a while after you've protected your position. You're practically an heiress to someone like

Jack, and you need to be careful."

His words had been unexpected, although I suppose it was a reasonable assumption when our situation was judged solely on appearances. I hated the words *someone like Jack.* He was the best thing to ever happen to me. I felt I had no option but to give Marcus enough information to reassure him and avoid awkwardness on the wedding day.

"I don't need a prenup. Jack is buying my brother's share of the house so we will own it between us," I said. "He's no gold digger, Marcus. Honestly, he isn't. My solicitor checked him out when we went to see him about the house. When everything is settled on the house, Charles has to pay me a large sum of money, and Jack is insisting it stays in my name, in my account."

I wasn't happy I'd had to tell him about our affairs, but I respected him, and I needed him to respect Jack.

Marcus thought over what I'd said before speaking. "I'm sorry for speaking my mind. I needed to make sure you weren't being taken for a ride."

It made me sad that someone as clever as Marcus would judge someone on appearances, just as my mother would have. The difference was Marcus had revised his opinion. That was something my mother would never have done. To be fair, Marcus had been looking out for me. Even so, I knew I could never tell Jack what he'd said.

We'd talked about asking the Wests, as well, but I feared they would have felt they were acting on behalf of my parents, and I'm sure Thomas would have expected to walk me down the aisle. It was too soon. It just wouldn't have felt right. After all they'd done for us, I hoped they understood. I did my best to explain it to them, and Thomas was as charming as ever.

We were married with the minimum of fuss and an abundance of love. The only pictures we have from that day were taken on Samantha's mobile and shared on a WhatsApp group made up of just the three of us. I loved those photographs. They captured the joy as well as the finest portraiture could have done.

Jack and I decided against booking a night in a hotel for after the wedding. All the hotels would be full of New Year revellers waiting for midnight, and that wasn't the atmosphere we wanted. Home would be fine, and, as always when Jack was in charge, there was a trip to the supermarket to buy in all the essentials for the celebratory meal he insisted he would be cooking.

Jack

I'd come home for the Christmas holidays because my mates were all busy with their women. I'd intended to find out more about my dad's family to see if I could claim to be respectable and had ended up marrying the girl who helped me succeed. Strange how things work out.

Charles had made sure we knew life was no fairy tale. Mind you, after all those years in the army, I had learned you have to grab happiness when it comes along, because life can't be taken for granted.

I couldn't call him rat-face anymore. That was his name when I thought he was just a nuisance. I knew better. He was a complete bastard.

When I got my visiting order to see Danny, he was more shocked about the whole Charles episode than the fact I'd turned up a married man. We'd grown up with lying rogues and thieves, but the premeditated murder of a sister for profit was on a different scale.

I'd taken him some prints from our wedding. When he saw Jo, he said just looking at her made what Charles had done so much worse.

"Who's he?" he asked, pointing to Marcus.

"He's someone Jo does some work for. He's a posh git. He really fancies Jo, but she won't believe it. You can tell by the way he's looking at her in the photo."

Danny studied the photo. "If I were you, I'd look at the way she's looking at you. You've got no worries there."

He handed it to me. For the first time, I concentrated on Jo's face, rather than the dopey look on Marcus'. Danny was right, as usual. I was shocked to see what I'd missed.

The news I was going to buy into Jo's family home impressed him. He knew the area, and like me, he was blown away by the thought of me living on the posh side of town.

"Man, I'm glad you're buying in," he said. "It stops anyone thinking you're taking her for a ride."

My brother still had his basic decency and would have hated the thought of me sponging off Jo. Of course, Danny didn't leave it there. "It means I can have the spare room whenever I want to impress a girl."

"The caravan's waiting for you," I said with a laugh, "in the bosom of our loving family."

"I'd rather sleep in the streets," he replied, laughing, too.

I changed the subject, and we talked about him. He was looking good and planning on getting the garage business moving when they got out. Leroy's cousin, Marie, was keeping it ticking over whilst they served their time. She was making sure it was completely above board and staying in profit, and she kept the two mechanics organised and in line.

Danny said I could go in with them when I left the army, and it felt good to know he was starting to look forward and still wanted me around. It was just like it always was. Danny was on my side, no questions asked.

"It won't be long now," he said. "Two years. Less with good behaviour."

"Then keep out of trouble so you get out as soon as you can." I was always scared he would take on someone's battles and end up serving extra time.

"You sound like an old woman," he said. "You look after your wife and watch out for her brother."

I didn't want to leave. It was always a wrench to walk away from him, and I knew he felt it too.

We assumed the whole buying-Charles-out plan had sunk, but we went ahead with the valuations and the survey and sent them on to Thomas West. We had heard nothing of Charles, and the police had never been back to us, so we presumed they were not charging him.

Out of the blue, Amanda made contact and wanted to visit Jo. I insisted on being there. There was no way she was going to bully my wife.

She was just as Jo had described her. She was immaculately and expensively dressed, and she looked down her nose at me. I could imagine how she had Charles completely under her thumb and made him feel grateful for being allowed to be there.

It was always going to be awkward, as it was the first contact we'd had since Charles had tried to murder Jo. She had never wavered from her belief her brother was ill, though. She was convinced he was under immense financial pressure and hadn't been responsible for his actions. She had always said, when it came to it, he could never have strangled her. She was sure it had all been an episode, a delusion, a fantasy, played out like some bad dream. I chose to disagree.

The only information Amanda could have had was from the police, because, up until then, she'd not bothered to hear Jo's version. Things didn't start well.

Looking directly at me she stated, "We will not be pressing charges for assault, even though Charles suffered significant bruising."

I was supposed to be grateful. I was brought up in

Atherton, and I had learned not to take bullshit. "It's my wife who's not pressing charges," I corrected, and enjoyed the shock that crossed her face as she heard the word *wife*. "If your crazy husband comes round here trying to kill her again, he's wasting his time. He's no longer her next of kin."

"Charles never meant to hurt Jo," Amanda said, her indignation obvious.

"That's exactly what Jo says," I said. "I disagree."

Just to make things clear, I went over his plot detail by detail. How he had signed in on a course in Birmingham, crept out, and taken the train to Tremby, getting changed on the way. I told her how he'd waited for me to go out, got himself inside, and then produced a cord to strangle Jo. I made particular mention of what he was planning to do to her after she was dead to throw suspicion away from him. I told her how he planned to catch the train back to Birmingham and return to the conference.

I watched her reaction and saw her turn pale. It must have been far worse than she could ever have imagined, but I didn't feel sorry for her.

"I came back, found Jo on the floor, covered in blood, with your crazy husband hovering over her. I grabbed him, pulled him off her, and thumped him to get to Jo. And, by the way, no matter what I say, Jo won't hear of pressing charges. She believes he had a breakdown of some kind, but I think he's just a murdering bastard."

"I think it has been brewing for some time. Surely you noticed he was behaving oddly?" Jo said, sticking up for her brother as she always did when I told it as I saw it.

Amanda did not go in for niceties. There was no shocked apology, no enquiry after Jo's health and no reply to her question. She just sat down, composed herself, and pressed on.

"I understand from our solicitor you want to buy Charles' share in the house. I've come to say we should go ahead as soon as possible. Charles has been sectioned, and I am using my Power of Attorney to see it through. I never expected to be using it in these circumstances, but I have no choice. At this moment, with Charles unable to work, I need the sale to go through."

Jo's reaction didn't surprise me.

"How is Charles? Which hospital is he in now?"

Amanda looked at her as if she had no right to ask, as if her questions were irrelevant to her. "I need to proceed with some speed," she said. "If we can agree on a price, there is nothing to hold us back." She started to produce papers from her bag. "Here is my proposal."

"You need to pass that to Thomas West," Jo said. "He will be negotiating on our behalf. It is a legal matter, and I want no direct part in it."

Amanda looked stunned. She had come there assuming she could make demands of Jo at will, and the realisation my girl had a backbone came as a shock.

"How are the boys?" Jo asked. "How much have you told them?"

"That's really none of your business. They're away at school, of course."

Jo sighed. Nothing changed. The woman had no thought for anyone.

"I'm glad you've got Power of Attorney," Jo said. "You need to look at the books and get a proper overview. I don't think Charles can support your lifestyle, so you need to check it out. I'm convinced he was planning to murder me to solve money problems. You may have to either cut back or ask your father for help."

Jo stood up to signify the meeting was over. "There is nothing left here for you to take from this family. Jack will be financing your buyout, not me."

She opened the door into the hall. Amanda had no choice

but to take her cue and leave. I opened the front door for her.

"Nice bag, by the way," Jo said icily. "I thought there was a waiting list for that one."

I had no idea what that meant, but Amanda clearly did. She threw its strap over her shoulder and glared at Jo. The point had gone home.

"What a cow." The words spilled from my lips as soon as the door closed. "He should have been getting rid of her, not you."

I put my arms round her and pulled her close. I breathed in that sweet, faint scent of hers and vowed to myself, once again, that I would never let anyone hurt her.

Ever.

Jo

Amanda proceeded quickly on our buyout of Charles' share of the house. Thomas West proved a worthy opponent, and he negotiated a fair market price for their third share and not a penny more.

I'd thought hard about letting them off paying me my share of the loan owed to my father's estate. My heart told me to forget it because they had hit hard times. Then I remembered how he'd tried to cheat Fi and I out of everything. He wasn't ill then, just a conniving weasel who dragged our mother off to make a new will under false pretence. I had always thought my mother would still have been alive if they hadn't duped her into taking a holiday with them. I decided I would accept the repayment, but it lay heavily on my mind. Jack thought I was mad.

I'd let Fi know what had happened. She was outraged. Fi never held back on speaking her mind and, on that occasion, she had plenty to say. I emphasised again and again he'd had a complete breakdown and had been sectioned. I had to try to maintain some balance over the whole sordid affair.

Fi was also forthcoming about my marriage. With the Charles incident, I hadn't got round to telling her until after the wedding. She had plenty to say about keeping it quiet, and I could only agree with her. I should have told her.

She feared it was all too rushed and was vociferous about Jack feathering his own nest, as she put it. I was able to tell her he'd paid for the wedding, every penny of the buyout, and all of the charges we incurred. I told her he'd insisted the cash Charles owed me was paid into my account. She calmed down a bit when she had time to absorb this information and said she would reserve judgment, begging me to take care.

It made me think. I'd found out my sister and my boss both thought I was a pushover. The strange thing was, I never had been. I'd chosen to look after my father, and I knew Jack was the man for me. I knew, when I had to, I could make my own mind up. Like I had about Charles.

Charles was detained in hospital for weeks, and Amanda eventually agreed I could visit. I was shocked at the change in him. He had always been wiry and sharp-featured, but he had lost so much weight he looked as if he had a consumptive illness.

Jack wanted to come along as my protector, but I didn't want any resentment and anger overshadowing our meeting. He waited in the car, a bundle of anxiety.

The meeting was brief but cathartic on both sides. I had no doubt it was guilt consuming my brother, and he admitted he had been terrified of facing me.

Neither of us could move forward without making our peace. I couldn't sugar-coat anything. What had happened had shaken me beyond anything I had admitted, even to Jack. However, it was important my brother knew, as far as I was concerned, he had not been responsible for his actions in planning to murder me on that awful day.

I think it was what he needed to hear me say. I'm not sure he'd received my message from his wife, and I could see in his eyes the relief my words brought.

"I'm a schemer, and I can be ruthless," he said, "but I'm not a murderer. I could see we were going broke, and I gradually lost it."

"I know," I said.

"I'm sorry, Joanna," he said, and then added, "for everything."

Again, his eyes told me all I needed to know. He was telling me he was sorry for all the cheating and all the spite, and I was relieved to hear it.

"Just get well," I said, "and leave the past where it belongs. That's what I'm going to do."

"Thank you," he said, and I believed he meant it.

When Thomas West had sorted out the buyout, we hadn't realised it was one of the last jobs he would do before he went into a full retirement. He and Lydia had a place in the Dordogne, where they wanted to spend most of their time.

They said Jack and I could visit whenever we liked, but we never did. It was one of those things we were going to do but never got round to it. We did keep in touch though, and it was good to know the two of them cared about us enough to invite us to visit.

We now owned my father's house together and could make it our home. I got used to being an army wife and the separations that came with it. One thing was sure, I never regretted my decision.

As time went on, Charles was discharged from hospital, and I was surprised when he took to calling in on me. I was never afraid of him. The shambling man who visited was far removed from my spiteful brother. I really believed him when he said he wanted to build bridges. As we talked, it struck me he was a broken man. Over the weeks we became more like brother and sister than we had ever been.

Amanda had done as I suggested and had gone through their books. She had then applied herself full time to making the business sufficiently profitable to meet their outgoings. Charles told me her parents had refused point blank to invest in the business. She, however, was sufficiently driven and sharp enough to succeed. She soon opened two further branches and went into the letting and property management business in a big way. She thrived in the commercial world as I'd known she could. She had the ruthless streak needed to succeed.

Charles wasn't well enough to go back to work back for months. He could see Amanda pushing the business forward in a way he never could, and his self-esteem suffered without her noticing. He couldn't bring himself to face their social circle and found himself isolated. I think that's why he took to visiting me. We chatted over cups of coffee in a way we never had before.

My brother accepted he'd lived his life trying to be the man our mother wanted him to be, a successful one mixing in the very best circles. After he married Amanda, he'd had the two of them to please, and he became the person Fi and I had no respect for.

I could see he was full of regrets. I didn't know if he still loved Amanda. He never said, but her success was hurting him. He said he envied what Jack and I had, and I wondered if he had ever known that sort of intensity.

He'd re-evaluated his relationship with his boys and was trying to forge a better bond with them. He said he wanted it to be like it had been between me and my father.

Jack never forgave him for what he'd done. Charles only visited when I was on my own to avoid seeing him. When the boys were on holiday, he would bring them over with him, and it was lovely to get to know them properly. It was humbling to see them with their dad. Though they were young, they seemed to know instinctively that he was emotionally damaged, and they treated him with genuine tenderness and concern.

I didn't see anything of Amanda. She never visited. After six months, Charles was able to do a phased return to work. He went to work in one of the smaller offices where he could try to forge a place for himself out of Amanda's shadow. It was hard for him, but he did it and learned to respect himself a little more.

His visits gradually decreased because he eventually worked full time, but we were both grateful we had had the chance to get to know each other properly. Fi was suspicious of his intentions at first, but she came to soften her view of her brother as she listened to my weekly news.

I still worked for Marcus. Jack wasn't keen on it, but it kept me busy when he was away. Marcus had the good grace to apologise for the way he'd misjudged Jack. I think he could see how happy I was, and he'd accepted I wasn't being taken advantage of. He was my friend, and I enjoyed working with him.

As all this unfolded, I discovered I was expecting a baby. Jack and I had wanted to have children quickly. Ben arrived screaming and kicking into our lives and within eighteen months, Oliver followed.

It was tough being on my own with them whilst Jack was away, but it was brilliant at the same time. I'd thought I wanted to be an academic, but I found out all I really wanted was to be a wife and mother.

Jack.

After four years, I was more in love with Jo than ever. I never thought I could ever be as lucky or as happy as I was. Things had turned out better than we could have hoped. We still couldn't get enough of each other. It was like an addiction for us both.

I no longer needed to park outside my father's house where Danny and I had once lived and think what might have been. I could drive right up to Jo's father's house and count my blessings that it now belonged to Jo and me, every single brick.

The house had worked out well. I never felt like a free-loader, because I'd paid my way. The small mortgage had been paid off. It was all ours.

We'd not really changed it that much, because we both liked it the way it was. We'd done up two bedrooms for the kids. Ben was three by then, and I swore he'd be an engineer one day. I'd never seen a kid take things to pieces so quickly and then try to put everything back together. He was always either building something or mending something.

He was my shadow when I was at home, and he used to keep up a non-stop babble of, "Didn't we, daddy?" and "Won't we, daddy?"

That was bloody fantastic. It was how I'd always wanted it to be when I had kids. True, if he fell over or was under the weather, only Jo could settle him, but that was because she's such a damned good mother.

Ollie was eighteen months old and was a cheeky little thing. He always tried to get his own way, though his only two words were dada and no at that time. We tried to get him to say mama, but he just wrinkled up his nose. Jo didn't worry about that. He howled if she left the room, leaving her in no doubt he needed her. She was busy trying to get him used to her temporary absences for his own sake.

Jo had finished her Master's by then and was due to start her PhD in the new academic year. It was going to be expen-sive, but we could manage with the mortgage already paid off. We both knew she'd always put the kids first no matter what. She was still doing bits of research for Marcus Burrows, and he paid good money. He wanted to give her more work, but we both wanted her at home with the boys. If I'm honest, I still thought he had a thing for Jo.

It had worked out all right for us with me in the army. Unless I had a weekend guard duty, I drove back from Catterick on Friday nights and left really early on Monday mornings to be back at camp for six. By then I was feeling it was time to give it up. I was missing out on so much with the kids. I was looking to quit the army at the end of the year to be there for them full time. I'd finished my degree, giving me a few possibilities for when I'd leave.

To be honest, I wasn't sure exactly what I'd do. Danny wanted me to buy in with him and Leroy in their garage business. By then, they'd got it back on track and were looking to expand. Leroy's cousin, Marie, had done a good job keeping it going for them, and they'd done wonders since they got out. It sounded interesting, but I didn't want to rush into anything.

Danny had come to dote on our boys. He wanted to give them all the things we missed out on when we were kids. That's why there was a six-foot teddy bear leaning against a wall in the garage. We had it in the house, but it scared Ben so much I had to get it out of sight. The battery-driven toy car next to it was waiting for Ben to be able to see over the steering wheel.

With Danny, it was all about spoiling them, and he couldn't wait to be able to take them to the circus and the fairs. He consoled himself in the meantime by taking Ben to the park on Saturday afternoons when it was fine. They always fed the ducks.

Ben would come back with something cheap looking and tacky, because Danny had once yearned for the things the other kids had when we were young. He was giving Ben what he hadn't been able to give me. Jo and I loved him for it.

At the same time, I was trying to give Ben and Ollie what I wanted when I was a kid. I wanted them to grow up in a house that was warm, and clean, and full of love. It was what Jo and I focussed on. Jo knew what it was like not to be wanted, just like me. I guess it was why we were so needy about each other.

Just when I was looking to wind things down in the army, I was told the me and the lads were being sent to Somalia in a couple of weeks for a four-month posting. We were going out to train the Somalian army to help them in their fight against Al-Shabab, an affiliate of Al-Qaeda. Just hearing those names struck terror in Jo.

She went into panic mode and spent hours on the internet. I told her she knew more about terrorist groups than Army Intelligence and MI5, and more about Somalia and its politics than the Foreign Office. This was one thing I couldn't get her to smile about. She was too scared, making me keep what I told her to her to the minimum. I didn't know much anyway.

I wished I'd got out of the army in the spring, then we wouldn't have had to face this fear. In the old days, folk believed in the wheel of fortune. Good times only keep going until you reach the top of the wheel, and then you hit the big drop. I'd had four years of good times, and this wheel of fortune thing kept niggling away at me.

Damn it, why couldn't I have ditched it along with all the other stuff I'd forgotten since I left school? I never did like English, so why this got to haunt me was bloody annoying. I didn't like hiding things from Jo, even when it was as daft as that, but she had enough to think about. It really played on my mind.

Chapter Six

Jo

I got the briefest of phone calls. The military base in Somalia had been shelled overnight, and Jack had been injured. They were going to arrange his transport home as soon as they could and would let me have the details as quickly as possible.

There were already stills on the net showing the scene and a report on BBC World News. I could see the base had taken a bad hit. There had been three deaths, giving me every reason to be thankful, but I was still in shock and despair. All I knew was his injuries were not life-threatening, and the impulse to ring for more news every hour was overwhelming.

I lived on autopilot for days, just waiting for Jack. I kept waiting to hear from him, to hear his voice. I tried his mobile constantly. It became a compulsion, but his number was always unavailable. It occurred to me it might have been destroyed in the shelling, but there was always the slight hope he would answer and I would hear his voice.

Danny was brilliant. In his own way, he was as terrified as I was, but knowing I was struggling, he came to stay and spent what time he could entertaining the boys.

Two whole days went past without news. I gave way and became the sort of wife to make the military despair. I was on the phone to them every few hours. Danny watched me but didn't try to stop me. If I'd not been ringing, he would have.

Eventually, I got news he was being flown home and

would be on his way to the Queen Elizabeth Hospital in Birmingham later that day. They finally confirmed he had a broken leg, and it needed surgery. I was relieved. It didn't sound too bad.

The names of the dead were released to the press that day, and Danny and I were totally stunned as two of them sunk in. James Tomlinson. That had to be Jimmy or, as Jack usually called him, Tommo. David Richardson had to be the one Jack always called Richo.

We knew then how devastated Jack would be. These were the men who'd joined up the same time as him. They'd stuck together like glue throughout training and in their placements. I knew both of them were married, and I felt sick at heart for their wives and children.

Danny volunteered to do childcare for a couple of days when Jack got to Birmingham. He took the time off work. I had no second thoughts in accepting his offer. He would die rather than let anything hurt them.

I drove over there as soon as I received their call. There was no use fooling myself. From the moment I saw him, I knew my Jack had not come back. His face didn't light up when he saw me enter the ward. There was no animation in his eyes, and although he stretched out his arms to hug me, there was no reassuring squeeze in response to mine.

From the first time, the first minute he had told me he loved me, I had never doubted I was as much the centre of his world as he was in mine. That day he greeted me as if I were some vague acquaintance. My common sense told me a visit from me could not counteract what he'd seen and been through. He would be reeling from the loss of his two friends. Maybe he had survivor's guilt. Still, realising the possible reasons for his reserve didn't help me face the rejection I was suffering.

I wanted to know everything, but I could see he didn't want to talk. I loved him too much to badger him for the information I needed to hear. I sat and held his hand. I told myself over and over to be grateful he was still here. It was horrible when he released my hand as if me holding it was irritating him. I had to fight tears when he turned to me and said he was tired. It was clear he wanted to be alone.

"I'll come back tonight," I said, leaning over to kiss his forehead.

"If you want," he said, and my heart sank.

I didn't leave at once. I went to speak to the ward sister, hoping I could get some of the information I needed from her.

She was kind and understood my concern about his state of mind. She reassured me it was only early days. I still needed to know he was receiving support for his mental state and badgered for answers. She told me everything was in place, and this was something they were accustomed to dealing with. She also promised he would get ongoing support.

I called Danny and told him how things were. He tried to reassure me, saying Jack just needed time. His words did not soothe me. He hadn't seen Jack.

I roused myself and showered in readiness for my evening visit. The eagerness I'd felt earlier in the day had gone, and it left an overwhelming emptiness inside me. I dreaded further indifference from Jack when I all I wanted was the old closeness.

He managed a smile as I approached his bed. It wasn't a Jack smile, but at least he'd made an effort. We managed to talk during the visit. He said he wasn't in any pain, even though his leg hadn't been set correctly in Somalia. His operation was due the next day. He would be discharged a couple of days after that. It was all very factual, but it was a start and better than the afternoon visit.

"You've been crying," he observed, as casually as if noticing my lipstick was smudged.

"It's been hard," I replied. I took his hand. "I've missed you."

"Me, too," he said, like someone who was delivering the expected response.

Jack was surprisingly mobile and had no problem getting in the car. His physical fitness meant that the cast on his leg—which had a walking heel—presented no difficulty.

"It's good to be out of there," he said. "It's stifling night and day. No fresh air."

"And good to be going home," I prompted.

He didn't respond, and my feeling of loss got a little more intense.

I had a hope that seeing Ben and Ollie again would reawaken the Jack I was missing. I'd told him their news. He had listened politely, but with little interest. I thought seeing them would be different. There was also the chance he would respond to Danny.

I couldn't wait to see the boys again. They'd had a lovely time with Danny, but it was time to have them back. At that moment, I needed their hugs and sloppy kisses more than I had ever thought possible.

The drive only took just over an hour, but it felt like an age. The silence was choking me. He paused as he got out of the car, and he looked long and hard at the house, taking in the welcome that it had always offered him.

There was a note on the table from Danny. He'd taken the boys out for the afternoon to give Jack some time with me.

"I never thought I would see this place again," he said.

I hoped that, somewhere, he was feeling glad to be back. The old Jack would have wanted to make love the minute the front door was closed, broken leg or not, but he made his way to his favourite chair and settled into it with a sigh.

He looked at me sadly. "I will try, Jo," he said, "but

everything's dark right now."

"We'll manage." I couldn't resist the need to throw my arms round him and kiss him. "I love you so much."

"I know," he replied. "I know."

A new phase of our life started where I pretended everything was lovely, whilst keeping the children from bothering Jack.

It was hard work. I cooked his favourite meals and kept him supplied with the endless cups of coffee he craved. I shuttled him to his physio appointments and counselling sessions with the children in tow.

I tolerated the endless, mindless TV he insisted on having on. He didn't want to talk, but he couldn't stand the silence. I don't think he watched a single program, though he did stare at the screen, and he didn't read the newspapers he insisted we have delivered. I was glad of them. In the evenings, when the children were in bed, I would read them and sit up late doing puzzles. It put off the moment when I had to go up to our room.

Bedtimes were painful. He lay with his back to me. I never knew if he was asleep or just pretending when I eventually went up to bed. It was lonely on my side, and I stopped trying to curl round him. The way he shrugged me off after a couple of minutes tore me apart.

I knew however hard it was for me, it was much harder for Jack. I could see the pain in his eyes, and knowing I could do nothing to make it go away gnawed away at my guts.

It was hard for Danny as well. He came most days on his way home from work, and I encouraged him to stay for dinner. It meant he and I could talk, and it was so much better than the silence across the table. He couldn't get through to Jack either, and Jack made it blatantly clear he preferred the television to Danny's company.

Danny was good, despite Jack's surliness, and would spend an hour playing with Ben and entertaining Ollie. It helped the boys to have his attention and our gloomy home temporarily warmed with their laughter.

Jack did start to go out after his plaster came off. He would disappear for a couple of hours and return in time for lunch. I knew he'd been for a drink, but he never seemed the worse for it, so I was glad for him. He was getting out of the house, and I was hopeful he was getting some company at the pub.

What I had not calculated was how much Jack could drink without showing the smallest sign of over-indulgence. We'd always enjoyed sharing bottles of wine over meals, but as a couple, we'd never been drinkers. I had no idea what Jack would drink when he was out with his army mates. If I had, I'd have been more concerned about his daily drinking. I was imagining he'd just been out for a pint.

It never occurred to me there would be a problem when I had to leave the boys with him whilst I went to the surgery for my smear test. I couldn't imagine leaving them in the waiting room, and I only expected to be gone for half an hour.

I popped Ollie down for his nap, knowing he would sleep for at least an hour and set Ben up with his Duplo.

How wrong can you be?

The appointments were running late, and when I did get out someone had blocked my car in. The receptionists were kind but could not locate the car owner. I leaned on my car to wait it out. Eventually, a woman came out of the hair salon opposite, walked across to the surgery car park, and unlocked her car.

"This is the patients' car park," I fumed, stating the obvious. "You've trapped my car."

She reviewed the positions of our cars. She had parked her car alongside mine, but within six inches of the driver's door.

The other side of my car was tight against a wall.

"You need to lose weight, you fat cow," she said, got in her car, and drove away.

"Classy," I shouted after her, annoyed to show my stress in public.

When I got home, Jack was fast asleep in his chair, mouth wide open. An empty whisky bottle was lying on its side on the floor. Ollie was screaming in his cot upstairs, and it was clear from the smell drifting downstairs he needed his nappy changing. Ben was in the kitchen and had got into the baking cupboard. He was sitting on the floor in the middle of a mountain of dried fruit, flour, caster sugar, and icing sugar.

"I'm making mummy a cake," he said, and he beamed at me with pride.

I had never raised my voice at Jack before, and I knew it was not going to help, but sheer frustration took over. I yelled at him.

He awoke from his drink-driven sleep and looked at me in astonishment. He couldn't register what was happening, but he knew I was upset. He roused himself from his chair, came over, and put his arms round me.

This was what I had been wanting since he'd come home. Yet it was such an empty gesture, and stinking of whisky, that I shoved him away.

"You can clean up the kitchen," I ordered. "I'll go and see to Ollie."

Jack

If I thought of my brain as an empty box and didn't let anything in, I could shut all the horror out. That's what they didn't understand. I'd have to release it to be able to tell Jo and Danny anything, and the terror would take me over. If they knew about it, they would talk about it, and I wouldn't be able to shut my ears.

I know I drove Jo mad with the television. I didn't watch it. I only stared in its direction and focused on keeping my head empty. I pretended I was watching to keep Jo, the kids, and Danny out. I knew I was hurting them. I could see it in their faces, but to open up to them was to lift the lid of the box, and I wasn't ready.

One day we were having a new double socket put in the kitchen, and the simple project was driving me mad. I knew we needed it. It was to let Jo use the mixer and the blender on the counter she used for baking, instead of struggling on the small space by the hob. We had booked it months before, but it was such a small job the electrician had kept us dangling whilst he picked up bigger jobs.

The banging and hammering set me off. There's no plaster board in this house, just solid walls, and the hole for the back box and the cabling channel had to be hacked out. I tried turning the television sound up, but it only added to the chaos raging in my head.

I left for the pub earlier than usual, glad to be out of the house. I don't usually drink spirits in the pub, but that day I felt I needed something extra to block it all out. I drank beer with whisky chasers and found my mood getting blacker.

I got ridiculously angry when I got home. The electrician had responded to an emergency and had left just after me. That meant he would be coming back the next day, and the hammering torture would continue.

Jo had made me sandwiches. She was still in the kitchen, just putting Ollie in his buggy, ready to go to the post office. Jo, my beautiful Jo, who, in that moment seemed to hold the power to release all this anger and tension seething inside my head. It was as if that box had become a pressure cooker, and the steam had to be released. At that moment, I could think of only one way to make that happen. A physical anger had erupted so powerfully it consumed me. I needed to punch it out of me.

I shoved Ben through the open door into the garden, and he looked at me as if I'd thrashed him, poor little soul. Then I pushed Ollie's buggy through the door and locked it.

It was hard to ignore the fear in Jo's eyes as she looked at me. It was as if she didn't recognise me.

It's easier to tell myself I don't remember the details, but I do. They will stay with me until I die. I could say I lost control, but that's a lie. I wanted to smash everything in sight. The release doing that promised to release the pressure in my head. In the end, Jo was the victim. It certainly wasn't about hurting my wife. She was just there, and I lashed out at anything in sight.

I'd be ashamed to even suggest she just got in the way as I smashed the kitchen up. I knew then her refusal to fight back was for the sake of the kids, but that makes me more ashamed. The banging and crashing must have scared them, but the sounds their mum made must have terrified them. She would have hated them hearing her screaming as I battered her.

The release of the pressure in my head only came after I'd smashed or pounded everything in sight, including Jo, and then I couldn't look her in the eyes. I skulked away to put the television on and slumped in my chair. The anger was gone, the pressure was released, but the walls of my box were breached. As the terror spewed out, all those images of mayhem and death were exposed. Shame and guilt flooded in, and the anguish was excruciating. I was alive and my mates were dead. I'd also beaten up the woman I loved more than all the world.

I don't know where she got her courage from, but Jo went upstairs to clean herself up without saying a word. She was quick because of the kids. She came back down in fresh clothes with her hair immaculate, a smile on her lips, and opened the door to let them in as if nothing had happened.

Both of them were crying and had been for some time. Ben had been screaming and kicking the back door and was hysterical when he came in. He threw himself at Jo and clung to her, sobbing. She scooped him into her arms and held him tight, telling him everything was fine.

"That electric man made such a mess," she said as Ben's eyes opened wide at the sight of Jo's battered face and the destruction in the kitchen. "I'll have to clear it all up. We don't want you hurting yourselves."

She cuddled them as she took their coats off, and she made them a drink. She would clear up the mess later. Just then, they needed her. She read them stories from their favourite books. Seeing the three of them, all curled up and safe with each other on the sofa, made me want to howl with shame.

Jo anticipated the usual visit from Danny that evening. When Ollie was having a nap and Ben was busy colouring, she cleared the mess and put a meal together for us all. She never looked at me once.

Danny is no fool. I can't blame him for realising I'd beaten Jo up. Her face was starting to swell, and bruises were coming through. One eye was nearly closed and the other totally bloodshot. There were angry marks around her wrists where I'd gripped her too tight.

He didn't even try to keep up a flow of conversation with me through dinner, although he was his usual self with the kids and kept making them laugh. After we'd eaten, he looked straight at me.

"Get your coat," he said. "We're going out."

Only Danny would have thought of driving over to Atherton and going back to our ramshackle old caravan. Showing more green moss than paintwork, it was lilting even more to one side. He had to put some force into opening the door and then signalled for me to go in.

He opened the front door of the house. "Me and Jack will be in the van," he shouted. "Keep your noses out."

He slammed the door shut, took his place on his bunk, and produced a bottle of cider from his coat. I understood then the brief stop we'd made on the way over. He opened the cap and took a swig.

"You and me, Jacky boy, need to talk, and this is where we do it best." He passed the bottle over to me, and I set myself on my bunk, just as I had done when we were kids. I took a swig of cider. The familiar, slightly sweet but dry taste took my senses back so many years a lump rose in my throat so big it choked me. How did Danny get to be so wise?

"Do you remember when you told me you were gay?" he asked, "and we had one of our talks? We need to do it again right now."

I smiled, despite my shame and the lump in my throat. "Your explanation of Santa Towels scared me to death about girls and so did our ghastly sisters."

Danny was right. It was time to talk. What should come first? The shelling and the explosion I'd been blocking out, or the violent attack on my wife? I drank from the bottle again. I needed to face both.

I started with the shelling. It had become easier to face than what I'd done to Jo. That afternoon had been the first time I'd looked back at it, and I'd only allowed myself the quickest glimpse. It had been enough. I was going to have to tell Danny about it, and it was going to be hard.

"We had heard shelling in the distance, but it was nothing new, so we carried on clearing up the training workshop, me, Tommo, and Richo."

Danny nodded. He'd known them. He'd been over to Catterick quite a few times since he'd been released and had enjoyed a few nights out with us.

"The one that hit came out of nowhere. The blast knocked

me backwards off my feet, and Richo landed on top of me, half his head blown away. Tommo took the full blast, and Richo and I were sprayed with his guts. Fire was taking hold and masonry was falling. A metal beam fell and shattered my leg. I thought it was all over for me, too, but our lads and the Somalis got to us really fast. They got us all out, what was left of us."

I'd told my story in a few sentences. I allocated myself those few words to convey to Danny everything I'd kept shut out, but he didn't need any more. He was shaking his head, and a shudder pass through his body.

"I went to their funerals," he said, out of the blue. "I didn't tell you, because we weren't talking about it, but I knew you'd have been there if you could. I just stood outside the churches. They were crammed full, so they streamed the service on a screen outside." He managed a grin. "I borrowed Leroy's suit."

My brother, the jail bird, the car thief, the one who'd looked out for me for years, had done that for me, and tears poured down my face. He'd managed to ease the guilt of missing their funerals, and I was grateful, more than he would ever know. I never loved him as much as I did right then.

"What happened today?" he asked.

Danny wasn't letting me off the hook just because I'd shed a few tears. He wanted more from me. It took me time to get myself together, but Danny was prepared to wait. We both had a couple more swigs of cider before I owned up.

"I lost my mind this morning. The electrician was hammering away at the walls, and pressure built inside my head. I went out to get drunk, but it made it worse. The pressure in my head built and built, and it got so bad I thought it would burst. I needed to release it. Like lancing a boil. I started grabbing stuff and slamming it to the ground. I needed to smash everything in sight, and Jo kept trying to stop me. She kept getting in the way. I needed to get rid of that pressure. I couldn't stop till I had."

"So, you kept knocking her out of the way?"

I nodded.

"You hurt her."

I nodded again.

He looked at me as if he couldn't believe what I'd done.

"I was like an animal. I must have thought smashing the place up would release the pressure."

"Jo got smashed up in the process Fucking hell," Danny said.

There really wasn't any more to be said. Danny was disgusted with me, and he certainly didn't want any details. He'd seen the evidence of the violence on Jo's face. I didn't want to even think about what I'd done, let alone talk about it.

The silence between us was unbearable. Danny, in his way, had loved me all his life, and he couldn't believe what I'd just told him. We sat there until we were both shivering with the cold.

"Let's go," he said. He drove me home in silence, but when he pulled up outside the door, he turned to me with anger in his eyes.

"Go and make it better if you can, but if you hurt her again, I'll fucking kill you."

He left me in no doubt he meant it. I slunk back into the house I loved so much like the rotten bastard I knew I was.

I crept up to the spare room, sat on the bed, and started to take my shoes off. The door opened, and Jo stood there, backlit by the hall light.

"Come to bed," she said.

She went back to our room and was in her side of the bed when I got there. I undressed and got in beside her, breathing in her scent of lily of the valley as I drew close. She took my arm and moved close. I didn't push her away or turn my back as I had been doing.

"Did you talk?" she asked.

"Yes." I couldn't comprehend her kindness, and it was all I could say.

"Good," she said.

"Jo, I'm sorry." A miserable response after all I'd done.

"I know you are," she said, and she kissed my cheek very gently.

"I hurt you," I said wretchedly.

"I know," she said, "I know." There was a soothing sound in her voice, maybe sadness, but no anger. "Try to get some sleep."

"Danny's going to kill me if I hurt you again."

"He won't need to," she replied. "Once was enough for me."

I knew she was telling me she'd never let me do it again, but I hoped she'd also been letting me know we'd be okay. I didn't know how we could be after what I'd done to her.

Her deliberate physical closeness to me told me I'd underestimated the depth of the love she had for me. I'd always known she loved me, but I'd never realised how much. She squeezed my arm again and then leaned over and switched off the light. That night, we slept curled in each other's arms as we always used to do, and it felt good.

Jo had phoned my counsellor, Sean, on his private number the previous evening whilst I'd been out with Danny. They had talked. I was grateful, because someone needed to be there for her. I certainly hadn't been, and it would have been too much for Danny.

She'd made me an appointment for the next day and had fixed up for the kids to go to a friend's house. She was able to drive me over and be there for me. I have to say Sean was first rate. Considering how deliberately ignorant and rude I'd been every time he'd seen me, he acted as if none of it mattered, and we started afresh.

God, I needed a fresh start, and for the first time, I answered his questions and engaged with him. After we talked, he asked if it was okay for Jo to join us. There was no danger I'd refuse. I think he wanted her there so she would absorb what he was telling me about what had been happening.

Jo's brighter than me, and some of what he said seemed to make sense to her and reassure her whilst I hadn't a clue what he meant. It was a bit too deep for me. Basically, what I did understand was I'd been in denial. Avoidance was the word he used a lot. I'd been drinking to help me block it all out.

He talked about survivor's guilt. I understood what he meant by that easily enough. Why were Richo and Tommo dead but not me? I'd been punishing myself for their deaths ever since I came to after the shelling. I'd cut myself off from everyone I loved, as well as keeping everything locked away. I'd kept my anger down until it got out of control.

He was optimistic things could improve, though he warned us now that I'd faced up to what happened, flashbacks were likely. He went through coping mechanisms with us. I paid attention to this. Maybe if I'd listened before, I could have headed off yesterday's explosion. More guilt to deal with, but after what I'd done, a bit more guilt hardly mattered.

Bless her, Jo hadn't known the details of what had happened in Somalia until Sean got me to tell her. I'd only told Danny. Even though I hadn't been able to talk to her until then, she was there for me, and after what I'd done, I couldn't have blamed her if she'd just walked away.

He asked if we wanted to talk about yesterday, there, in a safe place. Hearing the words safe place made me feel awkward, making me face once again the way I'd hurt Jo. It was a bit too touchy feely for me, but our home was no longer a safe place for her because of me. I nodded. It was the least I could do.

Jo spoke first. "It was horrible, and violent, and it hurt, but you weren't in control, Jack. All the time, I sort of understood your head was exploding."

Can you believe my wife? Her brother tried to kill her. She stuck up for him and said he was ill. I'd hurt her, and she said she understood why. I do not deserve her, and I'm scared one day she will realise it. I'm scared, too, that one day she'll buckle. No one can keep taking knocks like she has.

"I'm sorry, and I'm ashamed, and if I could turn back time, I would," was the best I could manage, totally inadequate but absolutely sincere.

Things gradually got better. The physio strengthened my leg, and it seemed fine. Sean, now I'd stopped acting like a dick, was able to help. I finally understood why he, being ex-military, got it. I'd never given him a chance before.

I started to face the survivor's guilt stuff and was beginning to accept Tommo and Richo's loss. Knowing Danny had been to their funerals helped a lot. Jo helped me write to their wives. It wasn't easy, but I had to do it.

I started to see my kids needed their real dad, and by shutting everything out, I had excluded them. I felt bad about that because I knew all about bad parenting. I'd not been thinking about them. I'd treated them as badly as Jim treated Danny and me.

It broke my heart when I realised Ben was scared of me. I was used to him being my little shadow, but he had started keeping out of my way. If I went to pick him up, he would shrink back from me. If I reached out to him, he shied away.

It was obvious to me by then Jo deserved the old me back.

I knew she wouldn't have the strength to keep propping me up indefinitely. At least, I'd started to try to find my way back to her, even though it was difficult. I hoped she could see how hard I was trying.

I decided the best way to show her we were going to be together for ever was to buy her an eternity ring for Christmas. I went back to the jeweller who had sold us our wedding rings to add to the meaning I was trying to pour into her present. The money didn't matter. The ring had to be perfect to symbolise everything she meant to me.

I was also trying to rebuild things with Danny. I needed him then more than I'd ever done. I knew how angry he was about what I'd done to Jo, but I hoped he'd see how sorry I was. I was never going to claim I hadn't known what I was doing. I'd known, all right. It was the most evil, selfish thing I've ever done.

The images of the lads at the end had burned deep into my brain and the flashbacks Sean spoke of were hard to cope with. They usually came when I was asleep, and I would wake up shaking and sweating. Jo was always there, and her reassurances pulled me back every time.

They occasionally hit during the day and paralysed me. I would see Richo with half of his face missing, smell the smoke and burning flesh, and see the flames getting nearer. I'd see the splattered guts of Tommo spewed all over us.

Thank God for Jo. She was there for most of them, and she would hold me and soothe me. It was hard for Ben if he was around when one hit, because the change in me scared him. I'd be cowering in a corner, shaking, with my arms over my head. Poor Jo would be trying to help us both, and I know she was being ripped apart each time.

He was having nightmares regularly. It scared me. I guessed they were the outlet for his troubled little mind when he saw me in the grip of an attack. He would wake up terrified, but never remembered his bad dream. Jo was the only one who could console him.

Danny was great. He took some time to calm down, but Jo helped him come to terms with what I'd done. How she managed to do it, I'll never know. I hadn't believed it could happen. What I'd done remained a guilty weight hanging heavily on my heart.

I was tormented by the oath I'd made when Charles had attacked her. I'd sworn I'd never let anyone hurt her. I had to live with the fact I'd smashed my own oath to pieces.

One thing was sure. I needed to get out of the army. Jo and I went through our finances. Jo did the calculations. She's much better at numbers than me. We'd paid the mortgage off way before I went to Somalia. With what I was going to come out of the army with, we reckoned I could take at least a couple of months to sort what I wanted to do. Whatever it was, it had to let me be based at home with Jo and the kids.

Eventually, as things improved, I got approval from the medics to go back at the end of November. I would be leaving for good at Christmas. It felt positive to have something to aim for.

Jo didn't want me to go back at all, but I'd worked it through with Sean. I needed closure. That's what he called it. I couldn't just leave when the last thing I'd done in the army was getting myself blown up.

Jo and I started planning for Christmas, which really bucked me up. Christmas meant such good things to us. We ordered the kids' presents and got them wrapped and stashed away whilst I was still home, and I had already got Jo's present. The eternity ring I'd bought her was wrapped and hidden in my bedside drawer.

I didn't get involved with the cards. No way! Writing them was always Jo's job. She had such lovely handwriting, and I hated writing.

I did organise the tree, though, and I insisted we wear our old festive jumpers to go and fetch it. We got the kids new ones. It was all set up before I went back to the army. There was a fair chance it would be bald by Christmas, the way the needles were dropping, but we didn't care. We needed to make a big thing out of it with the kids. It reminded us of our first Christmas.

To be honest, it was the first time Ben was old enough to get involved, and so most of the decorations were hanging haphazardly at his height around the bottom of the tree. It wasn't as perfect as we'd had it in the past, but it was more special than ever.

That night we shared a bottle of champagne in front of the fire, and we talked. We talked more than we'd done since I came back, and we felt our lives were more entwined than ever.

I felt sad as I switched off the tree lights before we went upstairs. An early start in the morning would take me back to camp and away from the cocoon we'd managed to rebuild together.

We made love over and over, right through the night, as if we couldn't get enough of each other. When I drifted to sleep, I felt happier than I ever had, even before Somalia had ripped our lives apart.

Chapter Seven

Jo

It felt awful without Jack in the house. I really didn't want to give him back to the army, but I could see he needed a positive end to his career, a closure he could accept and live with.

We talked every night, and I was angry when he told me he wouldn't be home for the first weekend. He had to go on a training expedition to North Wales. His leg injury meant he wasn't expected to do the overnight trek with full kit on his back, but he was needed to help set up the camp at the end of the trail. He was going by helicopter early on the Friday evening with the equipment and the back-up crew.

Jack was looking forward to it. It was just the sort of rough terrain he liked for camping, and as always, he was boyishly enthusiastic about the helicopter. Although I wanted him home with me and our boys, I could hear in his voice how much it meant to him to be back doing what he'd loved.

Ben was having his own adventure on Friday night, just like his dad. He was staying over at Danny's. I was as nervous about it, as he seemed too young to be going on a sleepover, but he adored his uncle, and I knew Danny would never let anything happen to him. He knew all about Ben's nightmares. Just thinking about them almost made me change my mind and cancel, but Jack thought a night away might help.

I'd put Ollie to bed and had poured myself a glass of wine and settled to watch a film. I was reflecting on how hard it had been to let Ben go off with Danny. It had been as bad as letting Jack return to the army. I was lost in thought when a news flash came on TV.

An army helicopter had come down in Snowdonia, and there were no survivors. The cause of the crash was not known.

I didn't care what had caused it. The TV had just informed me Jack was dead and would never be coming back. I was just absorbing it as Danny rang. He could hardly speak without sobbing, but he wanted to know if he should bring Ben back to be with me. By then, Ben was already asleep in bed. I said no, I wanted to be alone.

Alone. That was me from now on, and the wine I'd opened offered no comfort, no matter how many glasses I downed.

It wasn't long before the dreaded knock came on the door, and everything became official. My mother would have been proud of me as I served tea in the best china to the two officers. Seeing how difficult it was for them, I maintained a veneer of total composure. I tried to take in what they were saying, and they were very kind, but I was glad when they left. Jack was dead. What could they say to change that?

Like the obsessive housekeeper I am, I washed the cups and wiped everything down before I let myself think about going up to our empty bed. The timer had switched the Christmas tree lights on, and it looked more beautiful than I remembered.

I sat at its base. All the hopes and laughter Jack and I had shared when we fetched it and decorated it returned. All the memories of our first tree flooded back, and I started to howl.

I howled until my throat was raw.

The army does good funerals. That's what everyone said as Jack was laid to rest with full honours. His funeral even made the national news. Is there really any such thing as a good funeral when you don't want to let go of the one you love? When you'd rather be anywhere else in the world?

Danny and I felt distanced and alienated from it all, as if they stole our right to lay Jack to rest quietly. We were forced into an event neither of us felt comfortable with. It threw our private grief into the public gaze. We put on our bravest faces and got through it together.

We almost lost it completely when we were getting ready. I went to get Jack's cufflinks from his bedside drawer. I wanted Danny to wear them to his funeral as a tribute. It was then I found my Christmas present. The label said "To Jo. Together for all eternity. Love Jack.

His words broke both our hearts. Danny encouraged me to open it and we shed more tears when we saw the ring. I put it on my finger, and it has remained there ever since, along with my wedding ring. As I said to Danny, it really was an eternity ring.

Jack's family turned up in force, and they added to our stress. Neither of us had any desire to console them as their empty histrionics poured out. We hadn't invited them, but we'd anticipated they might turn up.

Samantha was with us in the family car, just as Jack would have wanted. She was absolutely marvellous with the boys throughout the whole day. She distanced herself from the wailing tribe and concentrated on our bewildered little boys. Most of the time she kept Ben distracted whilst she had Ollie in her arms.

Ben was in a daze all day. He knew his daddy had gone, and we'd tried to explain he wouldn't be coming back. Samantha protected him from the attention of the guests, and she wouldn't let any of her family near him. As she said, they'd never bothered themselves to meet him before, and they weren't going to upset him then. The funeral was a lot for a little boy to understand, especially such a sensitive one.

I'd told Fi not to come over. She'd only met Jack a couple

of times, and there was nothing she could do for me. Knowing she wanted to be there was enough.

Charles and Amanda were there. They deliberately blended into the crowd. Both knew how much Jack hated them, and it took real guts for them to be there. They'd brought the boys along, and they came over to give me a hug. Their boys sent Jack a wreath and brought flowers for me.

Danny and I got through the day. We shook hands with countless people and accepted their condolences. Their words were meant to give comfort, but they delivered none. He stayed over again that night, as he had done since he brought Ben back, and we shared a bottle of wine. It brought no comfort, either, but we raised our glasses to Jack and bade him a final farewell.

Danny and I were worried about each other's survival without Jack, and in the end, we decided Danny should move in with us permanently. Between us, we hoped to bring some sort of normality to the house for the boys. We wanted to give them, especially Ben, a normal Christmas. He was old enough to be looking forward to it, and we couldn't let him down.

Danny needed help to keep from drowning his sorrows, and I needed help to prevent myself from literally drowning in my sorrow.

We were perfectly aware of what people might say, but we were secure in our relationship with each other, and we didn't give a damn. Danny was the boys' uncle. They adored and needed him, just as much as he needed them. Danny and I were so traumatised by Jack's death we needed each other to get ourselves up in the morning and through each day.

I reflected on what my mother would have said to have an ex-convict staying in Charles' room. Strangely enough, it made me smile. How things had changed since she had ruled the place. It had been a welcoming home once Jack had moved in. Danny and I were determined it shouldn't become either a morgue or a shrine, as Jack would have hated that.

We fell into a rhythm that suited us. The boys and I gave Danny roots to keep him sure footed when all he felt like doing was getting wasted and giving up. The only rule I asked him to observe was not to bring women back. Danny was, as he had always been, an outrageous womaniser, and I didn't want the boys growing up seeing a stream of shallow relationships passing through the house.

I ploughed away at my PhD, collaborating with Marcus Burrows on research we could each use to our own ends. I was producing a thesis, and he was producing a tome which was to become the authoritative source for students of the Stuarts.

We kept his business running to finance the research and were picking up some substantial commissions. They were time-consuming and sometimes pulled us away from the research, but they kept us both solvent. Marcus was the rock in my work life just as Danny was in my family life.

Family was where Danny and I were strong. We watched the boys grow, and we worried over them and delighted in them. Ben was always a concern. He was quiet and serious, and he was still tormented by those nightmares. Though he could never remember or describe them, he would wake up screaming, and his terror took a long time to fade. In the end, our doctor referred hm on to a child psychiatrist.

The psychiatrist was patient and thorough but never really resolved the cause of Ben's fears or solved the mystery of the nightmares. He concluded Ben was traumatised by the loss of his father and the memory of his flashbacks, but was too young to comprehend or verbalise his feelings. The ed psych where the secondary school referred him reached the same conclusion.

Danny and I had worked all that out for ourselves years

ago and were anxious in case there might be something deeper going on. The experts found nothing, leaving us to support him as much as we could whilst trying to foster his independence.

He loved music, and I was the one who ferried him to his lessons and rehearsals. He played from a very young age. It was good to see him at the piano to appreciate the calm that came over his face as the music flowed from his fingers. He also played trumpet and became involved with a youth orchestra, which kept him busy and well challenged.

Ollie was far livelier. He joined the local football team as soon as he could, and he and Danny lived for Nottingham Forest. Ben wasn't interested in football, but Danny bought Ollie a season ticket as soon as he was old enough. They became a pair of pundits, monopolising the television when football was on, having an opinion on every referee, manager, and player to appear.

Ollie idolised and idealised his father, although he really had no memories of him. To Ollie, Jack was a hero who had died valiantly, and all he wanted to do was to join the army as soon as he could. He joined the army cadets and became a little peacock when he finally got his uniform. I wasn't sure it was good for him to have his dad on a pedestal in the way he did, but at least he talked about Jack, unlike Ben, who never mentioned him.

It worried me they were not close. Ben had no time for Ollie's military obsessions and his clumsy boisterousness. Ollie thought Ben was boring and a swot. Their love for Danny united them, and in that there was no competition. Ben didn't need a football-mad uncle, but he admired Danny's practical skills and his ability to repair the things Ollie accidentally broke as he rushed around the house. Danny saved many of Ben's treasures. Ben loved him for it and became his dedicated apprentice.

Danny stayed on, and eleven years passed by with us doing our best as a family unit. Jack was gone and I had two young sons to think about. It's trite, but life had to go on. It did at our house, which never had the same vibrancy without his warmth and humour.

The boys were our reason for carrying on, and we were as happy as we could have been, bringing up the boys and coping with the gaping, chasmic hole Jack had left in both our lives.

The boys had started school, and we went to endless nativity plays and concerts. I made their costumes, Danny made their props, and we were the loudest cheerers in the audiences. We were a team, Danny, the boys, and me.

The years flew by. Infants' schooling was left behind, junior school passed, and both boys were suddenly blazered adolescents, coping with secondary school. Ollie was outgoing and confident. Ben was shy and reserved, tormented by bad dreams. Danny and I agreed we needed to find a new way to address this, and Fi came up with a possible answer.

She paid a flying visit to England for a dental conference and picked up my boys on her way back to the airport. They were going back with her to the States to join her sons at summer camp. They were helping run the camp and would watch over my two.

It was part of a plan to help Ben's independence along. The cousins knew each other well from the visits Fi and the boys' made regularly, and Ollie was beside himself with excitement at the thought of a trip to America. Ben sometimes seemed to be looking forward to it, particularly the opportunities it offered for his music. Sometimes, because the poor lad was anxious about his bed-wetting but seemed to want the chance to get away from the dreams plaguing him almost every night. We talked everything over again and again. He was scared of making a fool of himself in front of others and terrified they'd learn he wet the bed.

We talked about how each time we'd been away on holiday the dreams had stopped. He'd never wet the bed then. He knew all this was true, and he also knew he had his night pants to rely on but feared the other boys might notice. In the end, he extracted a promise from Fi to rescue him immediately if it all proved too much.

Nothing reassured Danny or me. We had never been separated from the boys. Although we knew it would do them good, we didn't really want them to go. It occurred to us how neither of us had much of a life without them.

After they'd left, Danny disappeared into his parallel life. I wasn't worried about him. He'd really got his head together, and we knew he wouldn't hit the bottle or lose his way again. This drift was just how things were between us. We'd been a tight family unit for years, yet without the boys, Danny and I operated separately but totally amicably.

It was a good time to plough into my research, and I spent far longer than usual in the office Marcus rented in the town. He was putting in long hours, too, and it became a habit, when we finished for the day, we would go for something to eat. It saved us both from cooking and going back to an empty house.

There was something incredibly comfortable about being with Marcus. We had worked together for years, and he'd been a witness when Jack and I got married. He knew our history, including the hard time Jack had been through with PTSD. He had been understanding at the time when I couldn't guarantee I'd be able to work from one day to the next. He didn't know the full story, of course, but he had seen the bruises I couldn't hide. To give him credit, he had never asked a single question.

Jack had always been uneasy about Marcus, saying he

fancied me. Never, in all the time I'd known him, had Marcus given me any indication of it. I'd just dismissed it as part of Jack's love for me.

I'm not sure how it developed into an affair. It was more of a shift of emphasis as our meals together lasted longer and our conversation moved away from the research and on to more personal matters.

Marcus's willingness to share his story astonished me. All I'd known was his wife had died at a very young age from an aggressive cancer, and she had been a renowned scientist. I'd heard she had made a breakthrough in gene therapy early in her career and had gone on to achieve international acclaim. Apparently, in the months before her death, she was considered a likely candidate for a Nobel prize.

My father had told me Marcus must have been devastated when she died because of the way he walked away from his career at the university and moved into research. I'd assumed he was a grieving widower who wanted to work in isolation ever since my father told me his story.

Over one of our dinners, Marcus told me how her life had revolved around international conferences, lecture tours, and high-profile projects, meaning she had rarely been home in the later years. Having always believed he'd been stricken by her death, I was stunned when he told me he had not been as affected by her loss as everyone assumed.

They had tumbled into a relationship at university and married on a reckless student whim in their final year. They had realised, equally rapidly, it had only been infatuation and not love. Success came so quickly to her it promptly pulled her away from their shaky marriage.

She often had fleeting, inconsequential affairs with the colleagues she met as she criss-crossed the world with her work. She plunged into her liaisons recklessly but bored quickly and moved on without regret. He told his story without bitterness or rancour. They had fallen in and out of their entanglement, and both, being absorbed by their work, had not bothered to separate or divorce. He'd felt free to throw in his career after her death as she was no longer able to judge him for lack of ambition.

I couldn't believe I'd got his story wrong. I'd worked with him for years and had thought him tormented by grief. He brushed aside my apologies, saying he'd decided right from the start he couldn't go around saying it hadn't hurt much. He thought it would disrespect her, and he had no wish to do that.

I could see his point.

One night he asked me to his house for coffee. I can't pretend I accepted without being aware of what could happen. In truth, the thought of having someone's arms around me had become more and more appealing. I was missing the boys and felt miserable and alone.

His house was the starkest, most minimalistic place I'd ever seen. Scientific chic, he called it, with a hint of irony in his tone. His wife had worked on its design with the architect, and it was built to her spartan, clinical taste. Her early discovery in genetics had brought rich rewards, and she had invested much of them in the property. It was a monument to her memory constructed in concrete and glass. There were no carpets or curtains to provide sound insulation and our footsteps rang out beneath our feet on the solid floors. It was the clearly home of a scientist with no time for cosiness.

The only room with any comfort was Marcus' study. Arranged side by side, its crowded bookshelves lined the walls, and his ancient, battered, cluttered desk and worn chair looked inviting yet scholarly. The sagging and creased leather armchair suggested generations of avid readers had found comfort in its embrace. It reminded me of my father's study at home, and it endeared me to Marcus.

It was the perfect room for him, and it was clear he spent most of his time in there. His bedroom, in contrast, was functional and tidy but lacked character, and its huge, un-curtained windows appeared to offer no privacy. Marcus flicked a switch, and like magic, they turned to an impenetrable matt grey. Efficient, but clinical.

"We never slept together in here," he said as he showed me round.

I could not miss the underlying message. If we did sleep together, it would not be in their marriage bed.

"My wife had her own room and was very precise about when she wanted me to visit." He laughed. "She was also very specific about what she wanted when I did."

I looked at him with sadness. He had said little, and yet, I suddenly understood much more about his marriage and his life. I recalled the connection that had burned between Jack and I and realised once more just how fortunate we had been.

Marcus and I became lovers in a gentle, companionable affair. The biggest shock was to learn he had wanted me for years, from even before I met Jack. Until the boys went away, I'd never suspected he'd any interest in me. I'd never considered it because I'd never thought about him in a romantic way until then. It stunned me to realise Jack had been right all along.

I took a big step in entering into the affair. I had always thought there would be no one else in my life after Jack. I trusted Marcus understood what I was thinking, just as Jack would have done.

I spent most of the time at Marcus' place while the boys were away. Our house was too quiet without them. I imagined Danny had gone to stay with Leroy, as there was no sign of him at home. It was easier for me to be at Marcus' as he didn't seem keen on staying at our house. He said it still felt like my father' house to him.

I had no qualms about being with Marcus. I needed someone in my life just for me. I didn't mind looking after Danny and the boys, and Danny was a brilliant support for them, but something had been missing. Marcus was my someone and more besides.

We fitted with each other well in many ways because of our mutual interests. I hadn't had any culture in my life since my early student days, and I had forgotten how important it was to me. I had had many other priorities for so long, it was nice to luxuriate in it once more as we fitted in visits to the theatre, the ballet, and the opera. I was starting to feel like an intelligent, cultured woman again, rather than just a busy homemaker.

Marcus repeatedly said this was the best time of his life. Jack and I had a continual physical need for each other, a desire Marcus and I never had. When we made love there was no urgency, it was just leisurely and loving. This was a different sort of relationship, and I had no regrets. I loved the inner calm I got as I drifted off to sleep next to Marcus' steady breathing. When I woke in the morning, I liked to have him there to curl around and to feel his warmth invade my body.

There were practical considerations, of course. I had to call in at home to put washing through the machine and pick up fresh clothes. Danny was there on one of these visits.

He looked at me strangely as I went into the kitchen with my laundry bag. I was not prepared to try to pull the wool over his eyes.

"Have you been away? You've not been here whenever I've slept over."

"I've been staying with Marcus," I told him.

"Good for you."

I was grateful there was no hint of judgment there. I wasn't prepared for what he said next.

"I've been staying with Marie from the office." I must have looked at him in surprise. He added, "I think it's getting serious."

Danny had never been serious about any woman before. He had had more flings and one-night stands than he could remember, and I'd always thought he was commitment-phobic.

I'd met Marie when I'd had to take my car into the garage. She'd always chatted away as she'd taken my payments and dealt with the paperwork. I admired her. She'd run the garage efficiently for Danny and Leroy when they were in jail and had stayed on to run the office when they came out.

I'd always suspected she had a soft spot for Danny, but I'd never thought she stood a chance. I really liked her. She was homely, steady, and looked about ten years older than him.

"I'd like to be able to bring her back here sometimes," he said. "You know, I always envied what you and Jack had. I think I might be able to get close to that with Marie. I feel as if I need an anchor for myself. I'd like kids of my own."

He'd stuck to my house rules faithfully, and I realised Marie must mean something special to him for him to even ask if she could come round. I knew I didn't need to protect the boys from her visits. I was glad for him. He deserved a family and a life of his own after all he'd done for me, Jack, and the boys.

"Of course. It will be fine," I said and made a point of smiling. Danny needed to be comfortable in what had become his home. "I like Marie," I added, although he really didn't need my approval.

"I guess she'll meet Marcus when she comes," he said cheerfully.

"I doubt it. Marcus doesn't come round," I replied.

He looked puzzled. "Why not? Don't you feel ready to have another man in the house?"

I could see he was thinking of Jack. "It's not that. He prefers not to come here." It sounded odd, even to me.

"How does he feel about the boys?" Danny, as ever, had their interests in mind.

"We've never discussed it," I said, and at once I wondered why we hadn't.

I was hearing from Ben regularly. Less often from Ollie. I was glad they both seemed relaxed and happy. They looked fit and tanned in their video calls, and it was a relief to hear Ben say he'd had no bad dreams whilst he'd been away.

I mentioned this to Marcus as we cleared away after dinner, saying how much I was looking forward to having them home again. I saw him wince a little.

"I'm enjoying having you to myself," he said. "I've waited a very long time for this."

"They'll be back one day," I reminded him. "You'll have to share me."

"You're all mine tonight," he said. "Don't spoil it."

He was behind me and put his arms around me and pulled me close, nuzzling my neck. His breath was warm on my skin. "I'm no good at sharing," he said into my ear.

He picked up the wine and our glasses and headed for the door, turning back to make sure I was following. I was hesitating. His words had not eased my qualms.

"Are you coming?" he asked. "I have special things in mind."

For the first time, I followed him upstairs with misgivings. I came as part of a package, me and the boys. I had assumed he'd accepted it, but now I wasn't sure.

We began the last week we had to ourselves, and we still hadn't been honest with each other. The boys were on California time, and their calls tended to come through towards what was the end of the working day for us and breakfast time for them. They were both, in their own way, flourishing, and it was good to be able to relax about them.

While the bond between Marcus and I was strong, I sensed their return threatened our affair. I deliberately put my fears aside and carried on, staying over with him. In truth, I could hardly wait to be in his bed and was staggered by the way he could make me feel and respond. I was being selfish, and I knew I would have to face up to it all eventually.

"I'd imagined this would be our last time together," he said, "but I can't stand the thought of not being with you."

I sighed contentedly, thinking he was going to put his fears of my family ties aside.

"I suppose it might work if you could come over to me a couple of nights a week if Danny is still with you. Then you won't be worried about the boys." He spoke as if thinking aloud. "That's the only solution I can see working, but it won't be easy. I don't know how I'll cope with sharing you when I want to possess you all the time. I've waited for you for so long."

I knew he'd been uneasy about getting involved with my family, but I'd imagined he would at least have tried. Even though he'd made it plain enough I was important to him, he could not have hurt me more if he'd simply said it was all over. My anger rose quickly.

"You've known for the past fourteen years I'm a mother before anything else," I snapped.

This wasn't all about Marcus Burrows. First and foremost, it was about Ben and Ollie. "I can't see how that fits in with me abandoning them twice a week to come here to indulge your sexual fantasies." I knew it was crass of me to say it.

"Our fantasies," he corrected, and I knew he had a point. "Jo, I'm a fifty-two-year-old academic. I was never a normal teenage boy. I don't know anything about children. I can't be part of your family, as important as it is to you. Your boys would never accept me."

"They might," I said petulantly.

"I don't want teenage stepsons."

I should have admired his honesty, but it hurt too much.

"I thought these six wonderful weeks together were worth grabbing. Better than a lifetime of never knowing what we missed. I thought you felt the same. I couldn't imagine you wanting to share yourself with me once your boys came home."

"You never asked." The petulance was still there.

"I knew the answer."

"I wanted you and my boys. I thought you understood."

"I love you too much to wreck your life with those boys. I'm not father material. They'd come to resent me and you, and it would tear you apart."

A glimpse into the future, and a vision of Ollie's reaction to me trying to integrate Marcus into our household crept into my mind, and it chilled me. If I was being honest, I'd always known it would cause issues. Maybe I, too, had grasped the chance of six weeks with Marcus rather than a lifetime without.

"I don't want to be without you," I muttered.

"You know it's how it's going to be." Marcus looked straight in my eyes. "I think you always knew it."

It might have been true, but I was hurt and angry. We'd allowed no honesty between us all along. I was probably as angry with myself as I was with him. I felt weak and foolish and nothing like a woman of culture and intelligence.

At that moment, I hated what Marcus had made me become.

Danny was like an excited child the day the boys came home. He'd taken the day off work and was driving to

Heathrow to pick them up. I stayed behind to get things ready. I'd been cut off from practicalities and needed to head to the supermarket to stock up on food and get myself a very large dose of reality.

I was excited, too, but the excitement was tempered by my anger at Marcus and my disgust with myself. I'd have been far better off to have kept away from him and miss those weeks of indulgence.

The boys' return to the house eased the self-loathing a little as they had a lot to tell and show. It was impossible not to be carried away by their enthusiasm and impossible not to feel full of joy as the four of us sat round the dinner table that evening, just like we always had.

"Has Danny told you about Marie?" Ollie asked, mouth full.

I nodded, and Danny took over.

"Apparently it will be okay for me to see her as long as we still go to watch Forest."

"I'm glad you got approval," I was smiling but the words hurt. I couldn't imagine Ollie ever approving of Marcus.

"If it's okay with everyone, I'd like to cook Sunday lunch for us all and get Marie over to meet you."

"I hope she won't mind sausages," Ollie bantered, "or egg and chips."

I hope none of them realised all that was hurting me, especially as I tried to join in. "I have a particularly good wine that goes well with egg and chips," I said, and to ease the ache, took yet another large gulp of the wine Danny and I were drinking.

After dinner, the boys slumped with tiredness and went willingly to bed. Danny and I were left alone with our second bottle. Danny assumed we were both celebrating the boys' return and hadn't realised I was also drowning my sorrows.

"Do you think Marcus will want to come for lunch?" he

asked.

"Absolutely not." I knew my tone had been too sharp, but I couldn't help it.

Danny was too wise to pursue it and merely topped up my glass. "I hope you've got plenty of paracetamol in stock," he said, and raised his glass in salute. "I think you're going to need them in the morning."

I'm a mum before anything else. It's what matters most to me. They were my last thoughts I drifted off to sleep. Those words came starkly into focus a couple of hours later, when I was forced into consciousness by the sound of Ben's screams of terror.

Danny and I got to him at exactly the same time. He was terrified and shaking. Even after we'd put on the bedside light, it was ages before he focussed on us, and the terror started to recede.

I'd tried to sit beside him and put my arms round him, but he hadn't recognised me and had pushed me away as if I were a threat. He didn't respond to our voices at first, but eventually the panic left his eyes, and the dream faded.

It was good to be allowed to hug him and reassure him, and as he was in my arms, I was aware his racing heartbeat was gradually calming down.

Danny reappeared with mugs of tea for us, and we all sat together, sipping our hot drinks, and getting our thoughts together.

That had been one of the worst night terrors he'd ever been through, and we all knew it must be because he was home again. We knew he'd had no dreams whilst he was away, and it made it scarier because those dreams and terrors had to be linked to the house. None of us could understand what the link was.

The middle of the night with a frightened teenager was not the time for post mortems. We concentrated on reassurances and immediate solutions. Danny dragged the camp bed from storage in my father's room and fetched his duvet and pillows. He was going to bed down in Ben's room and keep watch until our boy could settle.

I went back to my room. When Ben had been younger, I used to take him back to my bed after one of his night terrors. It was sad but those days were long gone. I had to leave it to Danny.

As I lay there, unable to sleep, it occurred to me Marcus was probably right. He wouldn't be able to fit in with all this, even if he'd been willing to try. The only consolations I had that night was Ollie had slept through all the turmoil, exhausted by his flight home, and Danny had been there for us once again.

Danny was starting to think of moving away from us to create a home of his own. I didn't blame him, but it didn't make it any easier to accept.

Chapter Eight

Ben

I couldn't help wishing I'd never come home from the States. I loved my mum and Danny, but those dreams were driving me mad. If I could have remembered what they were about, maybe I could have got myself sorted out, but I couldn't. All I remembered was the terror.

Maybe my dad's issues had landed on me. I was going to go and see my dad's counsellor the next week. Mum had booked it for me. I never knew he'd needed one, but I'd started to think maybe his demons, whatever they were, were in my head.

Mum and Danny hadn't told me what they were, but they both said this Sean helped him. I hoped to God, he would help me because I couldn't take much more. It had been two months, non-stop.

I'd been thinking about the house and my dad. He was everywhere I looked. There were photographs in every room downstairs. They were starting to freak me out because he was always grinning at me. Maybe it was because he'd passed all his bad stuff on to me, and he was laughing at me. I'd started to hate our house.

It wasn't too bad when we were all together, but when I got to my room at night, I knew what was going to happen again, and I wanted to run away. I'd told Mum and Danny it wasn't as bad to get Danny sleeping in his own room again. It wasn't true. It was bloody awful. Worse than ever, but I felt such an idiot needing my uncle beside me to keep bad stuff away.

Ollie was getting on my nerves, too. He was being a complete twat, and he thought it was funny I wet the bed. He daren't make fun when Mum and Danny were about, but when we were on our own, he was unstoppable. At least, I'd got the bedsheets into the machine before he came down that morning. He'd have had a field day with Mum and Danny being out.

Danny had left at seven, and Mum had left at eight for London. She was going to see some documents at the National Archives for what she's doing with Professor Burrows. She said she wouldn't go, but I promised we'd be fine. She finally trusted me to get us both out for the bus and lock up.

I called up to Ollie again. I knew he'd be posing in front of the mirror, taking selfies. It was Remembrance Day, and the cadets were going to school in their uniforms. Ollie was obsessed by the army, and he idolised our dad.

Ollie had wanted to wear our dad's medals on his uniform, but Mum wouldn't let him. He'd worked on her for weeks to let him take them in for the Remembrance Display in the school foyer instead.

I shouted to him again. We were going to miss the bus at that rate. Whilst I waited, I took two paracetamols because my head was sore. The dreams had been worse than ever the previous night. When I woke up, I remembered nothing, but I was sweating and wet through, and my brain was going crazy, like a computer trying to retrieve lost files. It was awful, and I nearly went in to see Mum. Instead, I'd got the bed changed and thrown the sodden sheets into the machine.

I just wished I could have remembered what those dreams were about. They'd been trying to tell me something every night since I'd got home from the States, worse than before I left. It was strange how I'd not dreamed out of there. It had to have had something to do with the house and my dad. In a sudden burst of frustration, I rushed round and turned every photo I could find of him face down.

Ollie saw me doing the ones in the hall as he came downstairs. "What are you doing that for?"

"Can't look at him today." I had no other explanation. Let him make of it whatever he wanted. "Now let's go before we miss the bus."

I sat, as ordered, on a chair outside the principal's office, and I shook. I wasn't shaking with fear, and I didn't care what he was going to say to me. I wasn't going to say I was sorry. I wasn't sorry. It had made me feel better. All I wanted to do right then was talk to Danny. He was the only one who'd understand.

Eventually he opened the door, and I went in. I stood shaking, head down, in front of his desk.

"Why did you do it?"

"Don't know, sir," my lips said

In my head, I was saying, "*Of course I know, but I'm not telling you.*"

He raised his eyes to the ceiling. He was no fool. I hoped he would know I had my reasons for taking a baseball bat from the PE store and smashing the glass cabinet holding the Remembrance Display and then pounding at my dad's medals with all my strength. I guess it looked pretty anarchic.

It was complicated, and I was struggling to get my head round it. It was none of the principle's business. I'd been in the assembly, and we were watching a video of this big Remembrance event in London. At the end, poppy petals fell from the ceiling, one for every fallen serviceman. I realised one was for my dad. It came to me out of nowhere, like a punch in the head. I remembered what my dreams were about. My dad was just a vicious bully, and he didn't deserve a poppy.

"Ben, this is serious. I'm going to have to suspend you if you can't explain yourself. My secretary has tried to call your mother, but she can't get hold of her."

"You won't be able to, sir," I said. "She'll have her phone off. She's doing some research in London."

"We've managed to reach one of your emergency contacts and a Mr. Burrows is coming in to collect you. I'll make an appointment to see your mother next week. Until then, you will have to stay at home."

Shit, I thought. They have Danny's number. Why couldn't they have called him? "Professor Burrows?" I asked, aware as I spoke it wasn't the time to be picky.

"The only one on the list we were able to reach. Sit outside." He sounded disappointed with me. "Mr. Bacon will come and take you down to reception when your professor arrives."

Mr. Bacon was usually friendly, but what I'd done had really shocked him. He had to explain it all to Professor Burrows, and it was pretty obvious it was true. The caretaker was still sweeping up the broken glass as they talked.

"I haven't been able to reach your mother, so what should we do?" The professor looked ill at ease as we walked to his car. "Shall I take you home?"

The thought made me panic. Home was the last place I wanted to be. "Is there anywhere else?" I asked.

He nodded and strode off. I followed him, feeling awkward and bewildered. Things were worse than I thought, and the anger I felt towards my father was still fermenting. I couldn't think of him as Dad now. Dad suggested affection, and all I had right then was hatred.

"I think you'd better ring your uncle now," he said as soon as we were in his car.

I phoned Danny, but he still didn't pick up.

"We can go to the office and wait until you can get your uncle to come."

Danny was still not picking up, and I was demented by the horror that had flooded my brain. I needed to talk. It had been trapped in there for years, and once I'd remembered, it was driving me mad. I couldn't keep it in anymore.

Like a complete dick, I told Professor Burrows. He's my mum's boss. What was I thinking? The truth is, I wasn't thinking. I was spewing out the poison that was driving me mad. To be fair, he was a good listener.

I told him how my dad had come home one day, nearly thrown Ollie's pushchair in the garden, shoved me through the back door, and locked it. I'd tried and tried the handle, but I couldn't get in. It had started to drizzle, and Ollie was screaming, and my mum didn't come to us. In the end, I'd climbed on the garden seat under the kitchen window and tried to look through the blinds.

Not being able to see anything, I ran back to the door to listen. My dad was shouting, and I could hear the crashes as he smashed everything. My mum was begging him to stop, and he yelled at her to keep out of the way. After that I could hear her sobbing, then that stopped. Much later Mum opened the door and took us inside. She was hurt. Her face was a mess, and the kitchen looked like a bomb had gone off.

That was what had been trapped in my brain for years. I suppose I'd not been old enough to understand it, even though I knew it was something bad. I told him how the fear had got worse since I came home from the States. Sitting in assembly, it came to me, as clear as if it was happening right then.

For the first time, I remembered, and sitting there, I replayed the nightmare. I went out of assembly, fetched a baseball bat from P.E., and smashed the glass display cabinet to let me batter my dad's medals to smithereens. I needed to destroy them. He shouldn't have any glory after what he'd done to my mum.

Professor Burrows looked stunned as he heard my story. His face went grey, and I thought he was disgusted by what I'd done. I said I was sorry to him over and over.

"You've no reason to be sorry," he said, and there was something kind in his face and in his voice.

I started to cry, and I couldn't stop. I didn't make a sound, but rivers of water poured down my face. He handed me a handkerchief from his pocket.

"I'm going to try your uncle's number for you."

He held his hand out for my phone. I called up the number and handed it to him. Danny picked up.

"Can you come over to the office straight away?" he asked. "Ben really needs you."

He ended the call and smiled at me. "He's on his way. We can tell him the details when he gets here. Now I'm going to make us both a cup of tea. I think we need one."

It was a long time before I could talk to Danny about what had happened. It was all so complicated. He didn't press me to tell him. He just drove me home and waited.

I'd given Professor Burrows the outline, but I needed Danny to hear the rest.

I told him I'd got really stressed as the scene came back to me. I wanted to hurt my dad. If he'd been there, I would have battered him until his head was smashed in. I couldn't do that, but then I realised I could smash his medals up. I'd fetched the baseball bat.

Danny looked shocked when I told him how good it felt to smash up the display cabinet and beat hell out of those medals. Why should a violent thug like him have medals on display for everyone to admire?

He listened without interrupting me but wiped his face with his grimy mechanic's hands a few times as I poured it all out. I had the growing feeling he wasn't going to make it all go away for me.

Eventually, Danny spoke. "I always thought you were dreaming about your dad dying in that helicopter or maybe about the state he got in sometimes." He shook his head sadly. "You poor kid."

He fell into silence again as he thought about what to say. His arm was round me, and I waited for him to speak, resting my head on his shoulder.

"When your dad told me what he'd done, I wanted to kill him," Danny said, finally breaking the heavy silence between us. "I wanted to beat him senseless."

I knew then Danny understood how I felt. "Why didn't you?" I asked. I couldn't believe he'd known and let him get away with it. He'd just agreed that the nightmares told a true story.

"He was in such a mess I couldn't," he said. "He was pathetic back then."

"Nothing could excuse what he did."

Danny told me about Somalia, and about Richo and Tommo, and the shelling. He told me about the horror my dad had been trying to hide from and how it had all got too much for him.

All I'd ever known was my dad had died in a helicopter accident. What Danny told me was all new to me, and traumatised as I was by what I'd remembered, I was horrified at what my dad had had to face. The way Danny told it, I could almost hear the explosions and smell the burning flesh. To be honest, it was all too much to take in, but I'm glad Danny told me. It put what I'd remembered within a context I'd never been told of, and I needed something to make sense of it.

My terrors had turned out to be from hearing the struggle and the sight of Mum's injuries that day. The knowledge my father had done it to her was a ghastly reality, and it made me feel sick. It made me despise him no matter what he'd been through.

It was all a jumble in my head. Most of all, I felt rejected. My dad had picked me up and thrown me through the door as if I meant nothing. I'd hated being shut out and locked away from my mum. Just thinking about the frantic way I'd pounded on the door made me short of breath. Knowing I'd only been three didn't stop me feeling guilty I'd not been able to rescue Mum.

"Your mum always insisted he couldn't help it. She said he was completely out of his mind. She hated it, but it happened because of the terrible state your dad was in. She hoped the violence might release the tension that he'd been carrying around. She loved him so much she even said the bruises had been worth it to get his recovery started. That's what she'll say when you ask her about it."

That stunned me. "She talked about it with you?"

He nodded. "It was more that I talked to her. She wouldn't have said a word. Her face was swollen, one eye was completely shut, and her wrists were bruised. It was clear he'd hurt her. God knows what the rest of her was like. When your dad had told me what he'd done, I had to say something eventually. I thought too much of her to pretend I didn't know what had happened. She just shrugged it off, got on with things, and got your dad the help he needed."

It struck me then what an amazing woman my mum was.

"She understood where it had all come from," he said. "I couldn't. I still struggle. She knew how much your dad meant to me, and she knew he needed me to help him fight his demons. She made me get over it. She'll know how to help you. I'm sure she will."

"He hurt her," I wanted to argue. I wasn't ready to forgive. "He treated her like a punchbag."

"I know," he said. "I told you, I wanted to kill him."

"I wish you had." I meant it.

Danny wasn't much of a hugger. He was always awkward if Ollie or I tried to hug him, but that day he hugged me tight, and I cried like a baby in his arms.

I'd suspected for years I hated my dad without knowing why. I'd let everyone think I was sad because I missed him, particularly Ollie. I knew then for sure I'd heard him beat my mum up and seen her injuries. These buried memories had tormented me for years. I'd just got my head round it, and then Danny was telling me Mum thought doing it was part of his recovery process.

Danny's parenting skills would not pass most people's standards, but they were good enough for me. When I'd stopped crying, he went to the fridge, got two stubby bottles of beer, opened them, and handed one to me.

"I think we need this," he said and swigged from the bottle. "You know you've got to work out what you say to your mum. You have to tell her everything."

I took a swig and nodded. "I'll have to face Ollie. He'll know what I've done."

"You can leave Ollie to me," Danny said. "You just focus on your mum."

"I wish you were my dad." The words came from the bottom of my heart.

"One day you'll be glad I'm not."

Jo

When I left the National Archives, I had over twenty assorted messages and voicemails on my phone from Danny, Marcus, the boys' school, Ollie, and Ben. I sifted through them whilst I was in the taxi on my way to Saint Pancras and grew more and more alarmed. I gathered Ben had been excluded from school but none of the texts told me why.

Danny's voicemail explained what had happened. He didn't waste words. He said Ben had smashed the display cabinet containing the medals when he remembered his dreams were about Jack's attack on me. Panic surged through me. Ben would only have been three at the time.

How could my little boy have witnessed that horror? What would he be making of it, now he'd remembered?

Memories I had worked hard to forget came back into focus. Jack had shoved Ollie's pushchair through the back door and had pushed Ben out afterwards before he locked the door. Could Ben have listened at the door? It was all too possible he had heard his father smash up the kitchen. Perhaps he now knew his father had beaten me up. After all, he'd seen my battered face. My poor son must have heard me screaming and crying.

The sound of Ben hammering on the door and yelling to be let in resurfaced after all those years. Its noise filled my head and pounded in my ears. How could I have shut that out for so long?

Shame flooded through me. All these years I'd believed Ben's problems came from seeing his dad having those awful flashbacks. I'd thought losing his father so young and not coming to terms with his loss had made it all worse. It struck me then Ben's nightmares had been caused by what he'd heard when Jack shut the boys in the garden. It had never crossed my mind before. Had I blocked the possibility because I couldn't face it? What sort of mother was I?

Guilt poured in, creating a toxic mixture with the shame that wracked my brain. I shook as I sat through the train ride as if I was icy cold and shivering violently to get warm. All I wanted to do was to get home to my boy and reassure him everything could be made better. As I sat on the train, I thought of how he believed he'd had a violent father, and I needed to get back. He had to understand what had caused it to kick off that day. I hadn't gotten a clue how I was going to do that.

I got home at the same time as Ollie. Ollie was bursting with rage. He had his father's battered medals clutched in his hand. He beat me to the door, tore it open, and made straight for Ben, lunging at his brother

Danny stepped in and grabbed hold of Ollie, restraining his flailing attempts to attack his brother.

"Why did you do it?" he shouted.

"Let's leave Ben to your mum," Danny said. "You and I are going for a walk. We need to talk, and so do they."

I watched as Danny propelled a struggling Ollie through the door, and I have never been more grateful for his help. Only then could I look at Ben, tear stained and stricken. I opened my arms and within an instant my boy was in them, sobbing his heart out.

"I'm sorry," was all he could say, over again.

He had nothing to be sorry for, and I had no idea how to make him accept it.

Ben

How do you tell your mum you heard your dad smash up the kitchen? Or tell her you realised he had beaten her up because of the state of her face? I started with the dreams, the ones that upset me. I told her I'd finally remembered them, and it had made me go off my head.

My mum looked scared in a way I've never seen her look before. She took my hand and squeezed it, and she forced a smile.

"Tell me about your dream," she said. "Don't worry about me. Just tell me."

I told her. I told her I was sorry, but I was going to tell her exactly what I'd heard because she needed to know what I knew.

She didn't interrupt me. When I got upset and paused, she squeezed my hand again. It was hard to go on when I knew what I was saying was killing my mum.

"I hate my dad," I said. "I wish Danny was my dad. He'd never hurt you. Ollie thinks he was some kind of saint, and he needs to know he was evil. He didn't want us." I looked at her and tears poured from my eyes. "I think I just dreamt for years about him shutting us out and Ollie screaming. I'm pretty sure I only started dreaming about me yelling and pounding on the back door when I came back from America. I still couldn't remember them, but I knew the dreams were scarier. Then, when they came back to me, I lost it and went out of my head."

"Did Danny tell you about Somalia?" she asked, and I nodded. "We have to talk about the shelling, because facing it made your dad ill that day. It made him loose his mind. A bit like you did yesterday."

"I'm not like him." I sounded like a baby.

"You are," she said. "You're both sensitive, and bad things make you go a bit crazy."

"A bit crazy? He beat you to a pulp, and Danny says you think he couldn't help it."

My mum looked even more anxious as new thoughts struck her. "Did you hear me screaming? Did you hear me crying? I'm sorry if you did, my darling. I tried to keep quiet."

I nodded. She paused as she absorbed what I must have heard. Eventually she broke the silence. "What you heard must have been awful, but you have to understand, I think it was the start of your dad's recovery. He needed to release all that agony and tension in his head. Keeping it in was driving him mad."

She looked at me sadly and continued. "I'm sorry to be

blunt, but I want you to understand. Your dad loved me. Maybe I shouldn't have tried to stop him smashing the kitchen up. I put myself in his way. I don't think he realised he was lashing out at me. Nothing was registering with him that day."

"You can't know that."

"Yes," she said. "I can. No one will ever understand how much we loved each other, and you have no idea what your dad went through when he realised what he'd done."

"Not enough." I wasn't going to let him off so easily.

"He'd agree with you," she said. "I don't. I never will."

She put her arms round me and hugged me. I buried my face against her shoulder, smelling the sweet, flowery scent that always made me think of her.

"Your dad got better," she said. "You've got to get better, too. I'm sorry I didn't work it out. All this time I thought you were missing your dad and dreaming about him."

"What about what I did? I've got myself suspended. They might expel me."

"You need to think about it carefully. It will help you understand the state your dad was in when he let himself think about the shelling, and how he needed to get it out of his system."

I realised once more how wise my mum was. She understood why I battered those medals, and it made me feel better.

She kissed the top of my head and told me not to worry about school, she would sort it all out. At that moment, I believed her, and a bit of relief crept into my churned-up soul.

The relief didn't last long. Ollie and Danny returned. They'd been to McDonalds. Ollie had a milkshake in his hand. He looked at me as if he'd like to kill me.

Danny spoke first. "I've told Ollie how Ben has been dreaming about his dad smashing the kitchen up and you getting caught in the middle. We talked about Somalia and everything his dad went through. It's been really tough on Ollie."

Mum nodded.

"Why did you keep it all from us?" Ollie demanded. "He was our dad. We had a right to know what he went through. If you'd have told us, Ben wouldn't have had those nightmares. This is all your fault."

My mum looked so forlorn I wanted to shut Ollie up, but I'd done enough damage that day. I knew I'd only make things worse.

Danny took charge, as I knew he would.

"Me and your mum decided to focus on the good things about your dad. Why is that wrong? How is knowing he smashed the kitchen making anything better? Why is it your right to know he lashed out at your mum when she got in his way? Grow up, Ollie. Mouthing off isn't helping."

Ollie worshipped Danny, and being told to grow up by him came as a shock. He stopped his protests.

"Have you two eaten?" Danny asked.

We both shook our heads. Food was the last thing on our minds.

"Then me and Ollie are going to get you something amazing," he said.

He got Ollie out of the way on the pretext of getting supper ready.

Jo

Ollie went to school the next day, despite his protests. Students weren't allowed in the visitors' reception area where Ben had had his meltdown, so there had been no witnesses. The only ones who could have known would have heard about it from him. He needed to face it. He swore he'd not told anyone, but I wasn't sure.

We'd had a talk before he settled down for sleep, and I

realised what a good job Danny had done in helping him get his head straight. He was even feeling sorry for Ben by then and regretting all the teasing he'd done in the past.

He apologised to me, saying how hard it was to know what his dad had gone through in Somalia and afterwards. He admitted he only just felt old enough to handle it.

Danny had told him to grow up, and he was trying, telling me he was too old for his hug.

"You're never too old for a hug." I pulled him to me to say goodnight. He snuggled right back and stayed in my arms for longer than usual.

It struck me then I'd lost my carefree little boy forever, and I could have howled with the misery we had all had to face. I was thankful for Danny and glad he had Marie to prop him up at work the next day.

I made several frantic calls to Sean and got through eventually. He'd agreed to see Ben the next day when I told him what had happened. Maybe, knowing what the dreams had been about, Sean would finally be able to help get him better.

We were thinking of going for a walk as we waited for appointment time to come round when the doorbell rang. It was Marcus. The last person I wanted to see.

My brother had tried to murder me, and my husband had hurt me, but they had both been out of their heads at the time. Marcus had been very much inside his head when he'd decided he would only have a six-week fling with me before it even began. He'd betrayed me by not being open about it. I'd wanted our relationship to be more than a fling.

"I came to see how Ben is," he said.

"He's in a bit of a state right now," was the best answer I could give, trying to fob him off.

"I just wanted to see if there was anything I could do." He was clearly uncomfortable at my icy welcome.

A bit late for that. Had he handled things differently, we'd have been dealing with this together. A rebuff rose in my throat, but Ben appeared behind me.

"Come in," he said.

It was the last thing I wanted. My damaged boy, still in so much pain, took Marcus through to the sitting room and asked him to sit down. He asked me to make coffee, clearly wanting me out of the way. I lurked outside the room whilst the kettle boiled, straining to hear what Ben was saying and how Marcus would handle it.

"I wanted to thank you for yesterday," Ben said. "And I wanted to say sorry for dumping all my mixed-up stuff on you. I made a fool of myself."

There was a pause before Marcus replied. "You've been through hell," he said. "You have nothing to apologise for. I just wish I could have done more."

I was supposed to be making coffee, but I wanted to know what they were saying. I stayed at the door until I felt reassured.

"Ben, you need to trust me," Marcus said. "I'll never tell a soul what we spoke of yesterday."

"Thank you," my boy replied. "But I already told my mum and uncle what I told you. They needed to know you knew."

I was proud of Ben then and far less angry with Marcus. I went back to the kitchen, finished making the coffee, and felt slightly better.

I drove Ben to see Sean and forced myself to leave them to it. Ben didn't need me there. He needed to speak freely. I'd made an appointment to see the principle during their time together and braced myself to fight for my son.

"Mrs. Wicks," he said. "You have to realise how serious this is for Ben. It could be the end of his time here."

"It's Dr. Wicks, and I know how serious this is. I've come to make sure you realise what you're dealing with."

His face told its own story. Here was another doting mother come to protest what an angel their child really was. "Ben is with his counsellor right now."

Watching his expression. I saw no change. I guessed he was used to the psychologically damaged defence being trotted out by parents.

"Ben has been tormented by dreams and night terrors for years, as you may know. This school referred him to the educational psychologist when he was in year seven. It should be on his record. The intervention proved ineffective."

The principle nodded. I had no idea if he'd checked Ben's record or not. I hoped he had.

"You know his father died in a helicopter accident whilst serving in the army?"

He nodded again. His face assumed a sympathetic pose.

"What you won't know is my husband was injured by shelling when he served in Somalia, and he lost his two best friends. He returned home with PTSD. My boys never knew about it. We thought they were too young. Ben realised yesterday what he'd been dreaming about all these years and completely lost control. The dreams were about his father smashing up the house and attacking me. I'd absolutely no idea he remembered anything about it in any way."

I paused for breath. I'd tried to tell the story concisely and without drama. It struck me what I had said was enough to sink home to anyone with a modicum of understanding.

"Yesterday, not understanding what caused his father's behaviour, he was overcome with hatred for him. That is why he wanted to destroy his medals." I looked the head directly in the eyes. "Our job is to work out how to put my son back together and help him understand why his father did what he did."

"If we'd known . . ." His voice trailed off.

"Had I known the cause of those nightmares, we wouldn't

be having this conversation. I'd have understood what was tormenting my son and addressed it."

Mrs. Wicks . . . . sorry, Dr. Wicks, how do you want us to proceed?"

"I want you to strike the exclusion from Ben's record and accept he needs to be absent until we get him over this trauma. I shall see that he gets the support he needs, and I want support for him in place when he is able to return to school."

The head absorbed what I had said, and his face had abandoned its stock expressions for parental interviews and showed deep concern.

"What you've asked for is totally acceptable. We will, of course, provide work and online support for Ben during his absence." He must have seen my face darken. "When you advise us that the time is right," he added.

We parted on civil terms. I walked to the car shaking with relief. I was thankful that I could always find strength from somewhere when my boys needed me.

Ben's recovery evolved slowly as he came to terms with what he'd heard and seen afterwards. Sean helped. and to his credit, he also helped me without compromising Ben's confidentiality. Ben needed me to know he was struggling with his memories of what he still saw as a vicious attack. I had to accept that and not force my interpretation on him.

Danny was wonderful. He was particularly solid for Ollie, who was struggling as he adjusted to his new world view. He no longer saw the army as he once had, and he wanted to talk endlessly with Danny about Tommo and Richo. Danny was the right person. He'd known them both and could answer the questions I couldn't.

I was anxious that he was becoming obsessed with the morbidity of it all as he made Danny tell him about his dad's funeral and their funerals over and over. Sean agreed to see him, and this felt right. Ollie needed to understand it was as important for him to get help as well as Ben. He also needed to understand how hard it was for Ben, as well as needing support for himself. It had come as a shock to him that being in the army could involve real danger, and his dreams were destroyed. An accident was one thing, but warfare was another. What he'd learned of his dad's experience had affected him deeply. He was still angry with his brother for trying to destroy the medals, and he had to address those feelings as well.

It was tough for us all, but Danny and Marie did their best to bring some fun and normality into our house. That was when signs of the old Ollie would occasionally show through.

"Pity me and Ben aren't girls," he said one dinner time. "We could be your bridesmaids."

I checked my instinct to correct his grammar and joined in the laughter.

"Funny you should mention bridesmaids," Danny said. "Me and Marie are going to get married when we are all feeling a bit better."

"Why wait?" Ben asked quietly.

"Yes," Ollie chorused. "Why wait?"

I looked at them both with pride. Neither of them showed any jealousy or resentment over the way Danny felt about Marie.

"Because we need to find a house," Danny replied.

"Live here," Ben said, and Ollie nodded.

"I think Marie deserves her own house, don't you? You can't expect her to be your mum's lodger?"

"She'd be our aunt, not our lodger," Ollie countered, and we all laughed.

"We'll see," Danny said, "but I'm dead chuffed you'd want us."

That was that. Danny and Marie had both boys' blessings and knew they could move at their own pace without upsetting us.

I was acutely aware that day of how the house kept evolving. My father's house had changed from the days of my mother's cold regime to become warm and inclusive. People were glad to spend time there, except for Ben, who was still struggling at times.

There, we all were relaxed and happy to be with each other. Jack's once wayward brother and my soon-to-be sister-in-law were wrapped in its welcome, comfortable in its embrace, and loved by us all. I just prayed for the day when Ben would see what this house was really all about.

There was a tinge of sadness, too. I'd once hoped the boys could have eventually accepted Marcus and me in that way. He and I were operating on a business only basis. It was working pretty well, but not only had he hurt me, I missed him.

Marcus started to pop in to check on Ben. I challenged him about it when we were in the office, fearful he was using Ben to get close to me again, on his terms.

"You have no idea of the impact that day with Ben had on me," he said. "I want to help him if I can."

"You are qualified to help him because?" I could be a bitch when I thought I was looking out for the boys.

"We both love music. We both play the trumpet."

Ben had seemed to enjoy the visits, and I felt guilty when I recalled how I'd heard them talking about brass band pieces. I remembered how Ben loved playing from the album of piano pieces Marcus had popped round. Ben was always at his most relaxed when he played the piano.

"I was going to ask if it would be okay to get tickets for the Royal Marines concert," he said. "I won't if you don't want me to take him."

It made me feel even worse. "It's fine. I'm sorry, I thought you were using Ben's situation."

"You really don't think much of me now, do you?"

"I've got a lot on my mind with both boys. I'm over-sensitive."

He nodded.

The conversation had been uncomfortable, but there was nothing uncomfortable about Ben's reaction to the concert invitation. He'd been cooped up at home since the incident with the medals, apart from the visits to Sean and the walks we took each day. He leapt at the chance to go out.

My heart softened towards Marcus when Ben came home, dragging him into the house.

"It was fantastic, and when I said you and Ollie would love it, the prof said he could get tickets so we could all go together. Can we, Mum?"

Marcus looked uncertain, as if he was afraid of my reaction.

"They did Last Night at the Proms, and Ollie would love it. Please, Mum. It's been ages since we went out together."

"It's the prof now, is it?" I smiled at my boy. "Yes, we can all go. It will do us good."

It did do us good. Ben was right. Ollie did love the proms section, and I got emotional seeing them both singing their heads off and waving their flags. For the first time, it looked as if we could all come through this nightmare, and I was grateful to Marcus.

Ollie was buzzing on the way home. "I think I'll learn to play the trumpet," he said. "Is it hard, prof?"

"You should ask your brother," Marcus replied. "It's a long time since I learned."

"Have you got an old one I could borrow?" he asked.

"Ollie!" I cried.

"I'm only asking."

"Actually, I do have an old one."

"Then you could come round and help me get started." Ollie persisted. "I bet you're a really good teacher, being a prof and all."

Marcus laughed. "I'm a history professor."

"Same thing," Ollie said. "You know how to teach."

Somehow, the three of them sorted out that Marcus would come round on the next Saturday afternoon with the old trumpet for him and Ben to get Ollie started. Apparently, Nottingham Forest would be playing away, so it fit into Ollie's diary perfectly. Ben said Marcus may as well stay for dinner as it would mean I'd cook something nice.

My boys were back, maybe not permanently, but on the journey home they were as happy as I'd seen them in a long time. They went off to bed talking away like old friends in a way I'd been longing to see again.

I'd also got Marcus back, not as my lover as he had been, but as a regular visitor to the house. The man who had not wanted anything to do with my family had become one of their favourite people, and he looked happy to be with them.

The Saturday afternoon trumpet session was riotous. Ollie was not a natural, but he was as enthusiastic as ever. The house rang with laughter and musical discord. It was nice when Ben and Marcus played a duet to finish off their session. I realised how good they both were.

I'd made a curry, and Danny and Marie joined us. All of a sudden, the six of us were sitting round the table, laughing and relaxed. I don't think I'd ever seen Marcus look so at ease.

"Pity you're not staying over, prof," Ollie observed as Marcus restricted himself to just one glass of wine. "Danny and Marie are."

"Ollie!" Danny warned.

"The prof could have had more wine then," Ollie said,

feigning innocence.

"Maybe next time," Ben chimed in.

Danny and I exchanged glances. Did the boys have a new friend, or were they matchmaking?

"Then maybe you two won't mind if I take your mum out to dinner to thank her for this evening?" Marcus asked.

"Course, we won't," Ollie answered. "Better not make it too late though. She doesn't get out much."

Laughter rang around the table once more, and I found myself signed up to a date with Marcus that the boys approved of. I wasn't nearly as keen as they were. The hurt still lurked in my brain, and I wasn't fully convinced the boys were fully over their issues.

Marcus and I chatted over coffee the next time I was in the office. It was the first time we'd spoken since the dinner, although another music session had been arranged for the next Sunday afternoon. It was time to talk. We'd both been acting as if nothing had ever happened between us, and it was a strain.

"We plunged in too deep, too fast," Marcus said, opening up the conversation. He sighed. "I was selfish, thinking an affair like that could end when it suited me. I've learnt a lot since then."

He surprised me by admitting he'd been wrong.

"It's been hell without you, and I truly wasn't using Ben to worm my way back in with you. He really means a lot to me," he said. "Ollie does, too."

"I've missed you," I said, "but a lot has happened since then. I still think the boys have a long way to go, and I don't have the energy for us."

He nodded. "Ben especially has a long way to go. He talks to me."

To hear Ben confided in him hurt. He was seeing Sean, and

he had Danny and me. I think Marcus knew what I was thinking.

"Knowing how much you and Danny loved his dad, he can't really open up to you," he said.

"Of course, he can. He can talk to us about anything."

Marcus shook his head. "He can't tell you he still thinks his dad was a vicious bully and that you can't face what really happened."

It came like a blow direct to my heart. He was seeing Sean to get that idea out of his head, or so I thought. That was what would make him better. "He has to see," I said, panic rising. "I'll get Sean to make him see."

"You can't make him unthink what he believes happened."

He put his arms round me in a consoling way. I was grateful.

"Ben knows what he saw and heard, and he's old enough to make up his own mind about it. You can't make his anxiety about sleeping in his father's house stop because you tell him his dad couldn't help going crazy. It's going to take time."

He still held me, and I pressed my face to his shoulder. How did Marcus come to understand me and my family so well when I was floundering? Marcus, the man who'd abandoned me rather than face getting to know my boys. His role had changed. Like Danny, he'd become a rock for my damaged, little family, and I could tell he was searching for the right words. Eventually, he cleared his throat and spoke.

"Then, maybe we can put us back together," he added. "I've got as long as it takes."

About the Author

S D Johnson trained as a journalist but moved into teaching after her marriage. Her successful career ended abruptly after surgery failed to address mobility problems. She moved into the country and started writing full time. She has written poetry, a book of short stories, and is an active member of her local writing community. This is her second novel.

Printed in Great Britain
by Amazon

67592261R00108